Quince stopped strumming the guitar strings when he made out the vague shadow at the kitchen door.

Gradually he raised his voice, as though to make up for the lack of accompaniment. Then, with a sweep of his left arm, he whipped up the revolver.

Quince fired not an instant too soon, for the big man outside the door had stood with revolver leveled, the barrel gleaming against the black of his mask....

"He can wait now," Quince said. "There's a bullet hole through his heart."

SEVEN TRAILS was originally published by Dodd, Mead & Company, Inc.

Seven Trails

MAX BRAND

PUBLISHED BY POCKET BOOKS NEW YORK

SEVEN TRAILS

Dodd, Mead edition published May, 1949
POCKET BOOK edition published May, 1955
3rd printing .... December, 1971

This POCKET BOOK edition includes every word
contained in the original, higher-priced edition. It is printed
from brand-new plates made from completely reset, clear, easy-to-read
type. POCKET BOOK editions are published by POCKET BOOKS, a division
of Simon & Schuster, Inc., 630 Fifth Avenue, New York, N.Y. 10020.
Trademarks registered in the United States and other countries.

L

CONTENTS

1	THE PUPIL	7
2	GROWING OLDER	14
3	THE OUT TRAIL	19
4	"BAD LUCK"	27
5	YOUTHFUL GALLANTRY	33
6	UNDER THE STARS	41
7	FROM BEHIND A COPSE	47
8	A FIGHTING PHILANDERER	52
9	THE GHOSTLY WALKER	61
10	MARTIN AVERY'S STORY	66
11	A LONG-BLADED KNIFE	73
12	A WINDOW-SILL WARNING	78
13	"EL TIGRE"	82
14	JUAN GARIEN	88
15	AN EXCHANGE OF MESSAGES	93
16	WAITING FOR EL TIGRE	97
17	A PANTHER AND A BEAR	102
18	DON PETER SHOOTS	107
19	MUTE TESTIMONY	112

20 EN ROUTE 120

21 FAIRYLAND 126

22 THE JOKER 131

23 FACE TO FACE 136

24 FENCING WITH ANOTHER MARY 141

25 PETER MAKES A DECISION 147

26 A BRAVE COWARD 153

27 EL TIGRE RIDES ALONE 158

28 A TRUCE 163

29 A HAPPY MAN 169

30 JOHN QUINCY TALKS 173

31 THE REBUFF 180

32 AN AFTER-DINNER CALL 185

33 "STRAIGHT AS A SWORD" 189

1. THE PUPIL

PETER QUINCY'S mother died when he was four years old, so that all he could remember of her was really nothing. Yet he used to think, sometimes, that he could almost recall her features, and perhaps that was why, during the rest of his life, he looked so carefully and wistfully into the face of every woman he met. He melted their hearts with that look, like snow under a June sun.

After Peter Quincy's mother died, he was taken care of for a while by the huge man who tramped around the cabin in the mountains where Peter lived. Then one day a very old, very bent woman was brought to him. She looked him all over.

"He's a bad one. He's got a bad look in his eyes. He'll cause a lot of trouble in the world," said the old woman. "I would have knowed that that was your son, Quincy."

And the great dark-eyed, dark-headed man answered: "Mind your tongue, you old fool!"

But Peter kept looking straight into the face of the old woman until at last she opened her arms and gathered him in with a cry. It startled Peter and made him close his eyes for a happy instant, for it seemed to him that an echo of his lost mother's voice was in that cry. But then the withered hands of the old woman wakened him to the truth.

It was not very long after this that there came a rush of noise upon the house in the mountains, the calling of voices, the stamping of feet and the thundering rattle of guns. When the shooting ended, and the groaning began, strangers poured into the room, and someone caught Peter up by the scruff of the neck and held him out at arm's length. He was dangled before the eyes of a score of men. He would never forget how those eyes glittered, and how the guns shone in their hands; nor how the old woman lay twisted on her side in a corner, with her mouth open and crimson on her face.

"Will you look at this!" cried the captor of Peter Quincy. And he was clapped down upon a table, so that, standing upon it, he was as tall as any man. He looked them steadily in the eye. His father had taught him to do that with any man.

"He's got a look of my boy Tom that was stole away!" called someone from the background. "He's got a look of my boy Tom. By the Eternal, he *is* my boy Tom!"

The other men exchanged glances. And the man from the rear of the crowd, smashing his way to the front, caught Peter Quincy by the shoulders and peered hungrily into his eyes.

"No, no!" he groaned at last. "I guess my boy Tom would be a mite older than this, eh, boys?"

There was still no answer from the others; they had been killing a moment before, but they were melted with pity now.

"What's your name, son?" asked the man.

"My name is Peter Quincy," said Peter. "And what's your name, sir?"

"Peter Quincy!" cried twenty men at once. "It's the big devil's own son! Now who would have thought that there was bad blood in that kid?"

Two things never went out of Peter's mind to his death day. What the old woman and the stranger said was printed deeply in his memory, and, although he did not quite understand it at the time, he could recall it afterward, when he did know—he had bad blood in him, and his father was a bad man! When he was taken down to the village, people were continually stopping when he passed, and he could hear them murmuring: "No look of John Quincy about that youngster."

Whereat someone would answer: "Never can tell but one thing about bad blood—it's sure to show up sooner or later—mostly sooner, but always later on!"

How many things we say to one another over the heads of children, entirely deceived by their placid and dreaming faces. But they are acting a part all the while. They understand, and they are acting on a little stage of deception for our benefit. Perhaps they do not understand the words, but they are keen as hawks to pounce upon the lightest innuendoes. They can build a city out of a single stone, erect a monster out of a scratch on a rock and read the entire character of a man by the first word he addresses to them. In fact, very intelligent people are a little afraid of children. It is the shallow-faced contriver of games whom the children tumble over and dance around with shouting—and despise.

So it was with Peter Quincy. He walked on with a serene face, but in his heart of hearts he was revolving all he heard and all he saw. It made him very thoughtful; it also made him very deceitful. All children are marvelous geniuses as liars; the genius of Peter Quincy was stimulated, and while he was still hardly more than an infant he became a master.

He learned instantly, of course, that he was handicapped by having such a father as John Quincy. He also learned, in due course of time, that there were certain advantages connected with this relationship. For instance, when the boys cornered him in the schoolyard and taunted him with being a "pretty boy" and a "sissy"—oh, devilish taunts!—he had turned upon them at last in a fury, scooped up a stone in either hand, and behold! The entire group fled before him and took shelter with the teacher. And the teacher herself came out to him with great wide eyes and took the stones out of his hands and told him gently that he must never give way to such rages, because some day, if he struck another boy, he might—

This lecture on self-restraint was undoubtedly well conceived, and Peter Quincy listened to it with his blue eyes turned up to the face of the teacher in wistful eagerness; as a matter of fact, he was dwelling hungrily on the fact that he had been able to drive all the boys in the school before him. It was to Peter, of course, more than the possession of a gold mine.

When the report was brought home by the Andrews boys of what had happened at the school, Mrs. Andrews started up at the supper table with a cry and said to her husband: "Father, we got to have a little talk about things after supper!"

It was Bill Andrews who had hoped to see his missing boy Tom in Peter Quincy. It was Bill who had taken him into his home in spite of the fact that he already had two girls and four boys of his own and no overplus of income to support them. But where children were concerned, Bill Andrews had a heart large enough to take in half the world. This was an outstanding trait.

After supper the children left the table, and Peter Quincy, of course, along with the rest. But he came back with the secrecy of a snake, and, with an ear next to a generous crack in the wall, he heard all the conversation. It was a most important one to Peter Quincy. Mrs. Andrews was laying down the law sternly to her husband, and, being the mother of seven, of whom six were still with her, of course her husband allowed himself to be bullied. For to every father of a large family there is something miraculous about the wife. He may refer to her familiarly as "the old woman" or "the old lady," but this familiarity is merely an affectation, like that of the lion tamer, who shows a confidence which he is very far from feeling. He may impose on the public, but he cannot impose on himself. And, being left alone with his wife, Bill Andrews was sitting tilted far back in his chair, chewing nervously at the stem of his pipe, and regarding the floor just in front of his wife's feet, all of which Peter Quincy remarked.

The dialogue which ensued amazed Peter Quincy—or, Peter Quince, as the Andrews called him, to distinguish him as far as they could from that terrible outlaw, his father. For Peter, after he had been brought to the new home, had been quite neglected by Bill Andrews, whereas Mrs. Andrews had immediately taken him into her arms, wept over him, admired his beauty and mothered him to his heart's content. But now she was telling her husband with a savage earnestness that she would not have the "outlaw's brat" under her roof another moment. If he had turned on the boys in the schoolyard, he would turn on her own children one of these days. They would wake up one morning and find themselves all murdered.

Mr. Andrews found it advisable not to take any notice of this prediction. He pleaded with his wife soberly and earnestly. The boy had found a place in his heart into which he perfectly fitted, he declared.

"And our own poor boys go without a look or a word from you!" wailed Mrs. Andrews.

"For the Lord's sake!" cried Mr. Andrews, the perspiration streaming down his face. "Don't be crying, dear. I'll drive the boy out now. I'll take him and drive him out into the night. Poor little devil!"

And he rose to his feet. Mrs. Andrews saw him lay his hand on the knob of the door before she relented.

"We might as well give it a try," she said grudgingly. "We might as well keep him here till we can find another place for him."

And Peter Quince felt, rather than saw, the relief in the face of Andrews, as the good fellow turned away. But as for Peter himself, he knew now that the person to win in that house was Mrs. Andrews, and he set about that task the following day. A grown person might have been baffled by that task. For Mrs. Andrews was as shrewd as a Scotch lass and as hard as nails. But Peter reduced her enmity by half by straying through the fields on his way back from school the next day and bringing her home a great handful of wild flowers. And not a day passed after that without some such attention. In a week he was enlisted among those she loved, almost beside her own children. Then Peter, having won the fortress, diligently occupied it. But all of this was done with the most consummate naïveté.

Such was the simplicity of Peter Quince! But he lived for some years now occupied with a new fear. He had secured himself in a home, but what would happen when the boys, his schoolfellows, discovered that he was not a whit more formidable than themselves? Against the awful day of that discovery he began to make the most careful preparations. There was a one-eyed man in the livery stable who did the grooming and cleaned out the stalls. He was a negligible fellow; not that the West is cruel to the lame and the halt, but it has little time for sentimentality, and it does not give gentleness, except where gentleness is asked for. And no one would have dreamed of pitying "Sim" Harper. He had only one eye, and one leg below the knee was a wooden peg; these things were repulsive to the free-swinging cowpunchers, whose horses he cared for when they came to town for a splurge. Moreover, he was wrapped in silence day and night.

One would have said that such a man as this would have been impregnable, particularly to a small boy of eight, which was the age of Peter when he first met the stableman. Their friendship sprang from the following incident: In the first rose of a morning in late spring, Peter went in search of certain birds' nests, and so it came to pass that he was just under the window of Sim Harper when that worthy, dressing for the day's work, leaned out the window and let the wooden leg, which was in his hand, slip and fall. It fell into the very hands of Peter, and Sim Harper groaned. More than once that leg had been purloined by the crafty youth of the village, and he had had to hobble about the streets, hopping on a crutch, until he had bribed his persecutors to return the prize to him. He had a vision of a similar excursion this day. But, to his amazement, Peter Quince, unasked, climbed up deftly among the branches on the tree, swung perilously far out on a limb, and handed back the wooden peg. It was a tense moment.

Sim Harper said nothing. His thin, sour-featured face said no more than the silence of his voice. But Peter Quince understood. A child cannot be baffled, especially a child who, like Peter, has lived in the house of a stranger. Two days later, he dropped in at the stable and watched Sim grooming a horse—that rough grooming which is all that is necessary in the West. When the work was done they talked. And before they had talked half an hour, Sim had learned the secret wish of Peter, the desire which was nearest to his heart—and that was to be so dexterous and strong with his hands that the boys at the school should find in him, when he was finally cornered by some courageous spirit, a foeman as terrible as his borrowed reputation from his father made him. Of course, Peter could not say such things in so many words, but in a little while the story was out.

"Well," said Sim, "I'm right glad that you come to me. D'you know where I used to be before I got into that railroad smash?"

"Where?" said Peter.

"In the ring!"

He spoke with pride, throwing out his chest.

"What's the ring?" said Peter.

The other regarded him with pity.

"You dunno much," he said at last, "but maybe you could learn with teaching. Put up your hands!"

Peter obeyed the gesture as much as the words, as the stableman threw himself into the position of guard, with the stump of the left leg advanced, his left arm extended, his right fist back and poised for striking, and his little eyes glittering with excitement.

"No, no!" cried Sim. "That ain't the way! Put 'em up like me!"

Peter imitated the position to a hair.

"Now, hit me in the stomach."

Peter blinked when he saw that the invitation was seriously intended, and then he swung with all his might. But his arm was sharply tapped just at the wrist, his blow flew wide, and in return he was slapped smartly across the face. That retort stung him, and he darted in for vengeance. But wherever he struck he found the strong, bony arms before his fists. At last he staggered back, winded, but furious.

"I'll get at you yet, you crook!" shrilled Peter.

Then he saw to his astonishment that Sim was smiling.

"You'll do, old son," said Sim. "You just lemme show you a thing or two. If you want to hit me, start out this way. Put your weight on the ball—"

This was the beginning of the instruction of Peter. He was given one point at a time. There was no hurry, and Peter was very young. But in due process of time he learned that first of all mysteries, the proper use of the straight left, which is the rapier point that keeps the foeman at a distance, baffles his rushes, straightens him up and makes him a helpless victim—when the crushing right comes home. Peter practiced that thrust and learned how to throw all the weight of his lithe little body behind the blow, and how to lunge far forward and then recover with lightning speed. He practiced as carefully as the English yeomen used to practice with the long bow; or as carefully as young cavaliers of the days of duels labored over the intricacies of sword-play. The straight left was mastered. Other things followed. He learned that terrible and complicated punch, the right cross, which is delivered as the opponent lunges in, after his fist has missed. The right cross is a mixture of dancing step and bludgeon blow. Peter learned to step in lightly with his left foot, rising on his toes and then to sway down, coming flat-footed at the same instant that his right first jerked over the shoulder of his opponent and cracked against his jaw. He had to practice that blow by the hour, hitting over the hard arm of Sim Harper and checking the blow just before it landed. There were other things to learn—so many of them that Peter sometimes lost all hope. But Sim gave him just enough encouragement to keep him going. He learned the sway of the body which gives ripping force to an uppercut, and the convulsive jerk from head to toe which sends the whole weight behind a jab that travels only inches. He learned the complicated maneuvers which go with the shift, when the right hand strikes, as the right foot goes forward, and then the left hand with the left foot. He learned a vast deal about footwork, too, and was taught to glide, not to dance about, stepping smoothly here and there.

"For," as Sim used to tell him, "a good fighter does three-fourths of his blocking and half of his hitting with his feet. Get in an' get out with your feet, and when you hit, hit short and straight."

All these preparations went on for two long years, but when he was ten, Peter was tested.

2. GROWING OLDER

IT IS WORTH WHILE to give a picture of Peter as he was when he was in his tenth year. He had grown tall and slender. His face had lost its cherubic roundness and feminine beauty for a sharply chiseled handsomeness. But when he took off his hat, and one could see the pale gold of his hair contrasting with the rich blue of his eyes, there was still something unusual about Peter Quince; and though one could not call him feminine, he was a little too beautiful to be boyish.

His life had been calm enough. Mrs. Andrews was now his devoted slave, without knowing her partiality. He was cordially envied by the other children for the same reason, but he kept his place with the mother by a thousand cheerful little attentions, and he kept his place with the father by a pretended interest in the doings at the blacksmith shop. He learned to wield a light hammer and strike as hard as he could swing it in accordance with the directions of the tapping hammer of Andrews. He learned to tug at the bellows, and he managed to keep his smile and his bright eyes of attention through the smoke from the forge fire. So that Bill Andrews was charmed; for his own sons shunned and dreaded the shop.

Of course, Peter Quince had become an accomplished little hypocrite by this time. No one was allowed to come into his mind. He had no chums nor playmates. He dared not have, because if the other boys became too intimate they would learn that there was no native mystery or hidden strength in this son of the famous outlaw. And that mystery Peter struggled hard to maintain. Without it, he felt that he would be naked in the world. The Andrews family, he well knew, were glad to have him because there was something strange and terrible connected with him. Just as men sometimes take home a bull terrier in fear and trembling, but eager to show their manliness by keeping the king of dogs as a pet and companion. Peter had overheard neighbors complimenting Mrs. Andrews on keeping this scion of a man-killer; and he had heard her make light of the danger. But Peter Quince knew her inner mind, and he was not deceived. She adored him, as she might have adored a beautiful picture, and all the while she feared him.

To make the atmosphere of strangeness thicker around him, Peter adopted strange ways. He kept by himself. This made endless comment about his lack of boyishness. The other boys were sure to hear of it, and they were held back from trying him out by the dread of the unknown.

At least this was true until his tenth year, when a new boy arrived at the school. His name was Jack Thompson.

He was eleven years old, nearly as broad as he was long, and covered with muscles as hard as rubber and as strong. He devoted his first week to thrashing the older boys at the school. He devoted his second week to complicating the mystery of Peter Quince. And then on a fatal Friday night he attacked Peter himself, as soon as school was let out.

It was a gorgeous battle. Peter, white, trembling with fear lest the methods of Sim Harper should prove unavailing under the test of practical battle, met the first rush with an automatic straight left which fortune guided to a mark. And the first thread of warm comfort traveled through his veins, as he saw the rush stopped, and Jack thrown back on his heels. He stopped the second rush in the same way, and then stepped in, lightly rising to his toes, and whipped his fist over the shoulder of Jack with a beautifully timed right cross. It landed with marvelous precision on "the button"—that is to say, just to one side of the end of the jawbone—and Jack went down in a heap.

He was up again in an instant, hardly hurt, but Peter was walking away. Mere fighting would only prove him human, no matter how well he fought.

"Keep Jack away," he said scornfully to the others. "I don't want to hurt him."

And they caught Jack and held him away. The second straight left had split his mouth. It was only a scratch, but a crimson stain was smeared across his face and made him quite terrifying. And, while Jack gallantly struggled to get at his enemy, the other boys held him back and explained that he would simply be running into a stone wall.

So Peter Quince walked slowly away, shaking with relief. What would have happened had the battle gone on, he knew only too well. He might occasionally floor this stalwart youth, but sooner or later one of those swinging blows of Jack's was sure to land, and he would be broken in two. He had won; but his victory was rather moral than physical. Afterward he heard his foster brothers tell at the supper table, with bated breath, how Peter had thrashed the new terror of the schoolyard with three punches. It brought smiles of pride from Bill Andrews.

"That's what comes from learning to swing a hammer!" he said.

Peter did not dissent, but he knew better. When he saw Sim Harper, he generously gave Sim all the credit for his good teachings. But still he knew that even Sim deserved only a tithe of the credit. The real merit had lain in the use he made of his wits and not of his fists. Which convinced Peter, thus early in life, that battles should be won by cunning and strength, with cunning far the more important of the two elements.

All of these conclusions, of course, would have been harmless enough if Peter had been able to pass them on to a friend and confidant, but since he had no confidants, he digested the great idea in secret and at great length. It taught him once and for all that dissimulation was the way to success. He had praised two men for a success which he felt belonged chiefly to himself. They accepted the glory with much talk; he swallowed his own satisfaction in silence.

Naturally that was very bad for Peter. He should have spent his enthusiasm in chatter. But he went on smiling in one way and thinking in another.

Of course, all of these things are apart from the real history of what Peter Quince did and said when he grew up. But it is necessary that they be understood before that history commences. Otherwise, it would be too easy to condemn Peter. Whereas, as a matter of fact, he was really a victim of odd circumstances and a precocious mind. He was reasoning and thinking at an age when most children simply feel, eat, sleep. And no doubt the fight with Jack Thompson was as important in his life history and his character making as the fact that he was the son of terrible John Quincy.

There was one other great event which was necessary to complete the early education of Peter. It happened when he was twelve. On an early Sunday morning he found in the yard behind the Andrews house a ragged fellow, with an unshaven face and a broad, merry smile. He introduced himself as "Mississippi Slim," and, in return for the breakfast with which Peter Quince provided him, he launched into a long tale of wonderful places among the hills and wonderful adventures to be had in them, of sunny valleys where no one worked, of leaps across the continent by means of the railroads on which no tickets need be paid for. He built up so wonderful a tale that when he whistled under the window that night, Peter was out of bed in a flash, made up his bundle, slipped down the stairs and was gone.

He did not come back for a long nine months; and he came back lean and brown and more taciturn than ever. No one could get him to say where he had been, or what he had seen, or what had induced him to leave home. But now and again strange words and phrases left his lips. He seemed to have been in every state and every great city in the Union. He had stores of information about routes and railroads, from Texas to Montana and California to Manhattan. But no one could pump him for news. They could only guess at what he knew by words which he uttered here and there, and which were milestones pointing in surprising directions.

But he came back with one more thing which unlocked the hearts of the Andrews family and gave him his old place among them, in spite of his taciturnity, and this was a guitar, a weird stock of songs and a thrillingly sweet voice to sing them in. That boy soprano made the village, while it listened, forget that there was anything out of the ordinary in his descent. And he crowned his return to the community by an entrance into the village choir of the church!

Of all the sins of Peter in his youth, perhaps that was the worst. For sometimes, as he sang in the choir, with his lifted face and his shining-gold hair, it seemed to the dear ladies in the church that wings must surely be folded close under the robe with covered him. They could not guess that the emotion which shone brimming in his eyes was amusement at their profound admiration!

But now the education of Peter was practically completed. He had learned to fight men, to deceive men and to enchant them. The next step carries us far forward in the history of Peter, to the point when he was a mature man, and when events began to happen of such importance that they are worth recording in full.

3. THE OUT TRAIL

SOME MEN reach maturity on the first day when they leave the home of the father and start toward a family of their own. And others have entered their manhood when they first use their wits in business and win or lose. Some are men when they enter college, some when they leave it; but Peter Quince became a man when he discovered that the pursuit of a girl's affections can be made into a game.

No doubt it was not an estimable quality; but this narrative is not an attempt to paint a perfect hero. It is simply an effort to show Peter Quince as he was, with many sins and weaknesses, and with such virtues as chanced to be his. And how was Peter to feel the change from youth to manhood in another way? He had already, in his mere boyhood, done all the things which give maturity to the majority. He had left home and wandered across the continent. He had fought desperately with his hands. He had lived apart from others of his own age. He had been cut adrift from all support saving that which he could get with his own unaided wits.

There was no romantic leaving of the past and acceptance of the future when Peter Quince departed from the home of Bill Andrews to hunt his own fortunes. He had done it before, and the story was a twice-told tale for him. What made the great difference to Peter was the thing which antedated the leaving of the Andrews household and the direct cause of it.

He went to his first dance when he was seventeen. Not that he was without knowledge of how to dance. He had heard the strain of music for years, and the rhythm with its swings and its breaks had never failed to rouse a faint and rapid pulse in his veins. It made him happy for a reason which he could not discern, and when a youth is both happy and curious, he is excited indeed. And Peter Quince yearned mightily to go to the dance with the others.

19

He could not, however, without departing from the attitude of indifference to the other young people in the village which he had been forced into in his childhood, and to which he had religiously clung. For he was still known and pointed out as the son of John Quincy. The small change in his last name had not saved him from this. And at seventeen he was struggling just as hard to live up to his role as he had been when he was seven. Fists were no longer the only necessity. He worked a full hour every day, laboriously, practicing with revolvers. He learned to draw fast and to shoot straight. But that was not all.

A thousand others could do this. He must draw so fast as to baffle the eye which strove to follow the motion, and he must shoot straight and fast with either hand; otherwise, he would not be the true son of John Quincy. And, therefore, he got off by himself and worked faithfully every day. In the meantime, he kept apart from the others. His society was with older people—in the blacksmith shop, where he was now swinging the fourteen-pound sledge, shifting it easily in his stalwart arms; and in the church, where his high baritone was now the leading voice. But all the time he knew that this pretense at industry, this assumed sanctity, could not be continued forever. He must one day associate with those of his own age, and then—

As for dancing, he had watched covertly and studied the steps and practiced them, just as he practiced gun work. And at last the time came when he would need the training. He was lingering at the door of the church after a service. Almost everyone was gone. And in the sudden silence he could hear a group of girls talking near the steps outside:

"And Peter Quince?"

"Oh," said another, "Peter Quince looks like a real boy, but he's made of wood—he's a wooden man!"

And Peter heard them laugh in a pleasant chorus. It gave him a strange effect, that laughter. It tingled to the tips of his nerves and made his heart pound. It seemed to him that that laughter was like a fresh spring day, with newly come birds whistling around the housetops, and cloud shadows brushing across windows, and a chill in the clear air. He ventured a glance outside, and there he saw Mary Miller, laughing with the rest. It might as well have been any of the others, but he happened to be facing Mary and, therefore, it was her face that he remembered when he wandered on toward home a little later.

Mary was Billy Andrews' "girl." His face burned when he thought of that. No doubt Billy had told her everything he knew about his foster brother, and no doubt what Bill said had not been flattering. For Billy was a great ox of a youth who at twenty years weighed thirty pounds more than Peter Quince, and yet he could not handle the fourteen-pound sledge in his father's shop with half of Peter's ease and accuracy. He hated Peter for this and other reasons, and he was detested by Peter in turn. But, as Peter walked home this day, he found himself respecting Billy more than ever before. Even if Bill were an awkward fellow, he was undoubtedly strong of his hands, and he had at least been able to win the interest of Mary.

Her face haunted Peter. He had been wondered at and shunned and dreaded more than enough, but he had never before been mocked at. It angered him on the one hand, and, on the other hand, it made him a little afraid. For here was something against which he could not fight. If a young man laughed at him, he could knock him down. If an old man laughed at him, he could return mockery with ridicule. Even to an older woman it would be possible to talk back in a measure; but before a girl he was helpless. If they laughed at him, the only answer seemed to be a laugh in return. But how could he laugh without showing himself a fool?

What he felt finally was that it was very necessary to find Mary Miller again and talk to her. He wanted to be near her and discover if it were possible for her to laugh in his face. If she did, he felt that he was ruined. And that was how Peter Quince came to go to the dance. There was one that very night, and Peter, unheralded, attended it. That was not hard to do. It was not necessary to take a girl. There were never enough girls to go around, and the "stags" who attended the dances were usually as many as those who went with ladies.

But when Peter Quince stepped through the door of the hall, his heart was in his throat. He went quietly to a chair in a corner and sat down, wearing his most detached air of disinterest; but it took a concentrated effort even to partially succeed. He had been acting parts ever since he was a child, but he had never been more tried than he was now. The elders, who were there as chaperones and to dance old-fashioned waltzes in the corners, looked upon the coming of Peter Quince with the most utter amazement. The young fellows of his own age watched him with surprise; and the girls were dumfounded. He caused such a sensation, in fact, that he was given time to compose himself before it was necessary to talk.

How he chatted with a nearby matron, how he rose and was shown the dancing steps by her, he never forgot. Neither would he forget how the youth of the village watched and grinned. It was an unexpected pleasure, this privilege of watching Peter Quince appear as the awkward blunderer. They rubbed their hands in their glee. But Peter swallowed his chagrin and proceeded. He was apparently striking the colors of his dignity and self-completeness in the view of everyone; yet he managed to restrain his blushes and to laugh and talk with the utmost apparent good nature with the matrons who favored him with their dancing instructions.

And when he had stumbled through a few dances with them, exaggerating his awkwardness as much as he could, he went straight across the floor. Here Billy Andrews and Mary Miller were sitting together. All the time Peter was in the hall he had really been conscious of nothing so keenly as the presence of Mary. She had dark red hair and vivid blue eyes; but most of her prettiness consisted of vivacity in expression.

"Billy," said Peter, when he reached them, noticing that Mary continued to chatter all the time and paid no heed to his approach, "Billy, I was hoping that you'd introduce me to Miss Miller, and that she'd help me learn to dance."

Bill looked up at him with a mixture of anger and suspicion and fear. He had never known Peter Quince to be harmless before, and he shrewdly suspected that there was danger up wind now. Nevertheless, it was hard to refuse. And so, two minutes later, Peter and Mary Miller were dancing across the floor, and Peter was dancing with amazing smoothness, too. One would never have guessed him to be the same person who, a little time before, had been struggling through the measures with his middle-aged instructors.

"I thought you were above dancing," said Mary a little spitefully, as the dance began.

"I changed my mind," said Peter Quince.

"What made you change it?"

"When I saw you last Sunday."

"Peter Quince!" she cried.

"Do you doubt that?" said Peter, and he looked down at her with great, sad eyes. She studied them for a single instant and then glanced hurriedly away, as though she had been frightened. However, she danced very close to Peter and he decided that she was not unalterably estranged.

"But what I really want to do," said Peter, "is to have a talk with you. Couldn't we manage that? I have a great many things to tell you."

"What," said Mary, "have you got to say? Why can't you say it while we dance here?"

"The music keeps breaking in. Don't you understand?"

She did not speak again until they had swung around the floor once more, and were close to the door.

"Now!" she said, and, disengaging herself from his arms, she led the way quickly through the crowd and into the starlight outside, where other couples were strolling here and there among the trees.

"And now," she said, "what is it?"

He had not the slightest idea what he should say; and the only reason he had asked her to leave the dance hall had been to test what power he might have over her. Here she was; and what should he say?

"A little farther!" said Peter Quince. "Some of the others might hear."

"You're teasing!" cried the girl. "You haven't a thing to say, really!"

"Haven't I?" And he laughed, hardly knowing why. But he saw that the laughter did what words could not have done. It intrigued her to such a point that she could not hold back.

"You're so queer," she said. "What can be in your mind?"

"You," said Peter.

They reached a place which was solitary enough. Two shrubs as big as young trees fenced them away in a corner. By the starlight the girl became beautiful, and who would have guessed that a scant year before there had still been freckles on her nose? The heart of Peter began to tremble with excitement. He had brought her away for the mere pleasure of bringing, but now?

"Everything you do is so different from the others," she was saying. "And I couldn't believe my eyes when I saw you at the dance!"

"It was only because I couldn't stay away. I knew you'd be there!"

But he laughed to himself, for he knew that she was beginning to believe in spite of herself.

What a little fool she was, and what a double fool he had ever been to stand in awe of girls, if they were all like her!

"Do you know something, Mary?"

There was a change in his voice, and, as he spoke, she shrank away a little.

"What?" she asked breathlessly.

"When the starlight falls through the tree—"

"Well?"

"It makes you wonderful, Mary."

"You—you—you silly boy, Peter!"

"It makes me half afraid of you, on my honor!"

"Peter Quince!"

"But I mean it. Do you know what this is like for me?"

"You're going to say something foolish, Peter. But tell me."

"It's like a happy dream, and I'm afraid that if I stir or speak, I'll wake up and find myself back in the corner of the hall talking to Mrs. Burfitt."

She laughed very softly, the sound hardly escaped her throat, and there was such happiness in it that it filled Peter with a cruel wonder if he could really be the cause of it. So he decided to test her and stepped closer; then he took her hands, which were clasped loosely together. The fingers trembled under his touch, but they were not withdrawn, and it seemed to Peter that he had hold of something in her mind and spirit, also.

"You don't seem afraid of waking up now, Peter."

"I wonder if you're half as wildly happy as I am, Mary?"

"Where have you learned to talk like this to a girl, Peter Quince?"

"I wanted to say other things to you, Mary. But they've all gone out of my head. I've lain awake at night thinking out what I wanted to say to you."

"Are you speaking true, Peter? And have you really thought of me for long?"

"For months and months!"

"But you never even looked at me."

"I thought it wasn't honorable—because of Billy."

"Billy doesn't matter. Do you know why I've been so much with him? It was just because he could talk to me about you, Peter!"

"What a smooth little liar she is!" chuckled Peter to himself. "And Sunday she was calling me a stick!" He said aloud: "What has he told you?"

"A great many things, but nothing worth one minute of talking to you, face to face, Peter!"

"Mary!" called the voice of Billy Andrews from the distance.

"There he is now," said Peter.

"The stupid!"

"But he'll never find us here."

"I have to go back, Peter. Oh, they're beginning the next dance now!"

He loosed her hands. She ran a pace toward the building and then turned back.

"Are you angry, Peter?"

"I've no right to be angry; I'm trying to tell myself that!"

"Peter, dear!" cried Mary, and slipping up to him, she kissed his lips and was gone before he was aware of a figure standing in the deepest shadow beside the brush, and then the voice of Billy Andrews spoke.

"You mean sneak!" said Billy. "You mean, yaller hound!"

"Don't be a fool," said Peter, and he was amazed at his own coolness. "She was only practicing on me to get ready for you."

"It's your fancy way of talking that done the work!" snarled Billy.

It was one of the reasons he had always hated Peter. They had gone to the same school for the same length of time; and because Peter had learned "teacher's English" and kept his G's intact for the most part, Billy felt that an unfair advantage had been taken.

"But one of these days," said Billy, "somebody is going to stop that tongue of yours from wagging."

"You talk like a fool," said Peter, and yawned in his face.

The result was unforeseen. Billy was not the most peaceable fellow in the world, but who could have dreamed that he would reach for a gun in such an emergency? That, however, was exactly what he did. The long Colt flickered at his hip and balanced in a steady line but before it could explode the gun of Peter had been conjured forth from his clothes. It was his weapon which exploded, and Billy spun about with a gasp and dropped on his face.

He was not badly hurt. By the time the people came running from the dance, the guns had been put away, and Billy was able to tell how he had shot himself by accident while fooling with his gun. They bandaged him and carted him home, but Peter Quince knew that the end of his home life had come. He could not stay in the same house with Billy after this. In fact, he did not want to stay there. For there were other girls in the world like Mary— like her, but far more charming, and he must take the out trail which would lead to them. So he went to Mrs. Andrews the moment she was away from the bedside of her son. He found her with a face set as cold as ice.

"Billy has told you everything, I guess?" said Peter.

She did not answer.

"I've come to say good-bye," said Peter.

"Murderer!" gasped Mrs. Andrews.

So Peter went to his foster father, and in the darkness of Bill Andrews' bedroom he told him everything. The blacksmith considered it all for some time, after his habit.

"Peter," he said at last, "I'm sorry to see you go, but I'd be a pile sorrier to see you stay. That ain't for our sake only, because it's in you to fly higher than you could fly with us. And if you don't fly high, you'll fly low and go to the bad, and I ain't anxious to have my boys go along with you."

With this, Peter went to Sim Harper and waked the old fellow in his bed. Sim lighted a pipe and heard the tale.

"It's the left that does the work," he said at last. "Don't forget that, son. When you get in a pinch, keep that left going, and when you've got an opening, finish 'em off with the right. Hit short and hit straight and do your blocking with your footwork."

He put on his wooden peg, grunting over the straps. And he went down to the door with Peter.

"One of these days," said Peter, with a lump in his throat, "I'm coming back for you, Sim, and I'll take you to a place where you can finish your days without working."

"Hell's bells!" roared Sim Harper. "Am I as near dead as that? Good-bye, boy, and God bless you!"

So Peter went off down the street on foot, for he had not even a horse to ride, and all his earthly possessions he could easily hold in his two hands. They were stuffed into his pockets; his face was turned on the out trail; and out of all his years behind him he regretted only two human beings—Sim Harper and that man whose face he had forgotten—John Quincy.

4. "BAD LUCK"

HE WALKED to the nearest railroad, which was a simple matter of twenty miles. He made that distance by dawn, and he proved to himself that he had not lost any of the cunning which he had accumulated in that long nine months of rambling across the country and north and south from city to city. He slipped onto the rods, rode out the division that day on them, dropped off at a mountain town in the dark of the evening and went foraging. It had been a matter of honor with Mississippi Slim to "batter" the doors of the largest houses only, and Peter Quince followed that example, except that he was too proud to beg. Instead, he skirmished in the rear of the big mansion at the head of the one street in the village. It was a turreted structure of the mid-Victorian school, and, doubtless, it belonged to the rich man of the town.

Peter Quince climbed to a second-story window like a monkey, and entered. He had to have money and he had to have food. He found money in a room near the front of the house. There were twenty-five dollars. Peter took the cash and left in its place his Colt, which was worth fifty. He made his exit through the rear window, just as he had entered and, all unconscious and regardless of the fact that he was now a house-breaker and liable to a long term in prison, Peter Quince strolled down to the hotel, bought and ate a hearty meal and strolled on through the night.

He slept five hours in a haystack that night. The rest of the time he was walking, for the night was refreshingly chill, and the stars were bright, and the mountain air was wonderfully sweet with the breath of the pine trees. He came in the dawn to a charming little valley, with a stream twisting brightly through the center of the hollow, and a fine scattering of big trees here and there. There was a hut in a clearing, with smoke rising calmly, until it cleared the tops of the trees, when the wind tossed it away to nothingness at once. That smoke spoke volumes to hungry Peter, but what spoke still more eloquently to him was a white horse in a corral near the shack; for the instant Peter saw that horse he knew that it belonged to him.

He went straight to the fence and leaned over to examine his horse. He was as sure of possessing that mount as though he had the bill of sale for it in his pocket at that instant. Such a feeling as that comes to men rarely, and to the lucky ones it comes only once in a lifetime, and then they see the horse which is for them perfect. It fits into their minds like the last block into a picture puzzle. And they are happy on the instant and never stop being happy as long as the horse lives. For the horse is theirs. If a murder has to be done to win the horse, the murder is committed, and there is no qualm of conscience afterward. If theft is necessary, theft is performed.

All of this knowledge came to Peter Quince, as he leaned there upon the upper rail of the fence and stared at the horse. It was an iron-gray, and he was so white and so beautiful that he seemed to Peter Quince like a great mass of living, quivering flame. He stood an exact fifteen hands and three inches; and he was so muscled that when he stood still he seemed slender, and when he moved he seemed a Hercules of horses. But why describe him? Peter Quince could not think of details. All was an exquisite outburst of music in his heart. And if he noted the small, square muzzle and the flaunt of the tail, which suggested airy speed like an eagle's, it was all done in a haze of pleasure. He regarded the stallion in a mute ecstasy for half an hour, and when he was done he could not have described a single feature of the animal; but he felt that he would have known the very beat of its hoofs in the distance.

Then he glanced up and saw that he was being watched. As a matter of fact, she was standing almost opposite him. Her sleeves were rolled up to the elbows; in one hand she carried the milking stool, and in the other hand was the pail of steaming milk, the sight of which made the stomach of Peter shrink with the violence of his hunger. In the near background the cow was waddling off toward the day's pasturing.

"Do you mean to say," said Peter, "that you have milked that cow, and that I haven't seen you?"

"All right here under your nose," she said. Then she laughed at him so joyously and freely, with her head thrown back, that his ear and his eye delighted in her.

"You've been too busy watching 'Bad Luck.' How long have you been standing there?"

"Is his name Bad Luck?" asked Peter Quince.

"Yes, Uncle Dan calls him that. And he's right. Things have gone wrong ever since Bad Luck arrived on the place."

"Well," said Peter, "there'll be a change before long. He's my horse, you know."

She had a smile in readiness, quavering uncertainly at the corners of her lips and trembling even in her throat, on which the morning light was shining.

"But I mean it," said Peter. "Bad Luck is my horse!"

"Don't let Uncle Dan hear you say that," she warned him. "Uncle Dan has a terrible temper."

"I'll talk to Uncle Dan then."

"But not about Bad Luck."

"Why not?"

"It throws him into a passion to have him mentioned."

"Of course," said Peter, "you know your uncle better than I do."

She sighed. "You'll be staying to breakfast, Mister—"

"Peter.

"Peter, without the 'mister,' Miss er—"

"Mary," said the girl, and they laughed together.

"I'm starved," said Peter.

"I'm glad!" said the girl. "I mean—but you understand."

"Of course. Come here, Bad Luck!"

"Don't let him come near you. He's a terrible fellow. He thinks nothing of flying at you with his teeth, or trying to drive his heels through you, and hardly anyone has ever been able to ride him!"

"Watch!" said Peter.

He leaned and picked a handful of grass which he held out to the stallion.

He had not the slightest fear. He knew just what the horse would do, as surely as if he had read the book of destiny, and he was smiling at the girl, not the white horse, as Bad Luck came to him and took the grass daintily out of his hand.

"Oh," said Mary, "you're a magician."

"If that's magic," said Peter, "I am. Good boy, Bad Luck!"

He rubbed the white forehead. The stallion came nearer and nibbled at the brim of his hat.

"I can't believe my eyes," cried Mary.

"No one has ever trusted him before," said Peter. "They've always gone to him with whips and spurs, I'll wager. Come here beside me and try him."

She obeyed, but the instant she stretched out her hand, Bad Luck flattened his ears with a squeal of anger and snapped at her fingers. She shrank away with a scream, while Peter ran his arm around the neck of the white horse and looked back to her, shaking his head with wonder.

"I don't understand it, then," he said. "But I knew that we understood one another—Bad Luck and I!"

"When Uncle Dan sees this, he won't know what to say."

"Does he generally have words for everything?" asked Peter, as he picked up the bucket of milk and walked on toward the shack with her. She glanced sharply up to him.

"Do you know Uncle Dan Thomas?"

That was all she needed to say to prepare him for what was coming—that and the dilapidated condition of the hut in which they lived. Yet he was a little startled when he encountered at the door of the shack an immense man with a tumbled shock of black hair, who was filling a before-breakfast pipe and yawning the sleep out of his bloodshot eyes.

"Who in thunder is this?" he grumbled at Mary.

"Peter."

"Peter what?"

"Peter, a hungry man," said Peter, and he smiled on the monster.

"There's no spare chuck in this here house," said Uncle Dan Thomas. "Trot along, son."

Peter hesitated. He could see that the girl was biting her lip with mortification and displeasure, but he could also see that she had not sufficient courage to speak again on his behalf.

"I can pay for the meal," said Peter, "if that makes any difference."

"Lemme see the color of your money," said the big man.

"Uncle Dan!" cried the girl.

"Shut up!" he commanded.

Peter obediently produced the bills from his pocket. And the other scowled down at the coin through the cloud of smoke which he sent up in lighting his pipe.

"Put in a couple of more eggs and a couple of slices of bacon extra," he commanded Mary, and with this oblique invitation he strode out through the doorway past the girl and her guest.

She was crimson with shame, as she passed inside with Peter, and she had just raised her eyes to his in ques-

tion, when a deep-throated roar boomed from the outside:
"And mind that there ain't no talk about me. I ain't going
to stand it! I'm old enough to get treated better, and I'm
going to stand up for my rights!"

"Oh," murmured Mary.

"You're short on wood," said Peter with the utmost good
nature: then, picking up the ax which stood in the corner,
he sauntered outdoors.

There he attacked with an extra vigor the log which
was being worked up into firewood. Long labor with
sledge-hammers had tempered his arm muscles to steel,
but there was an added zest in pouring into the ax work
the anger which he felt at Uncle Dan Thomas. He had to
get rid of that anger, if he expected to be able to
execute and even conceive some scheme through which he
might get Bad Luck.

The big man drew near to watch the work. "Handy
with an ax, kid," he commented.

"Thanks," said Peter, and sank the shining blade inches deep in the hard wood. He had to wrench it out
with an effort which almost snapped the handle.

"All young men are young fools," said the amiable
mountaineer. "They's enough weight to any ax to do its
own work, boy. You can't show off your muscles to me.
Look here!"

Without more apology, he snatched the ax from the
hand of Peter and assailed the log. And, in fact, his work
was a marvel of efficiency and grace. The chips flew in
a ceaseless and regular rain, great chunks bitten out by
the slicing of the steel, and yet the strokes were delivered
with the most perfect ease and grace. In a moment, it
seemed, he had eaten his way through the log twice and
then split the chunks into firewood size.

"There," said he, "is the way to handle an ax. But none
of the youngsters know nothing in these days!"

And, so saying, he hurled the ax from him. It went
wheeling through the air with terrific speed, and yet it
was flung so cunningly that the bit struck squarely in one
of the logs of which the house was constructed. With this
exhibition, Uncle Dan Thomas turned with a scowl upon
his companion.

"Could you do that, boy?"

"That," said Peter, "is wonderful!"

And his great blue eyes were bright with the admiration with which he looked upon the other.

5.   YOUTHFUL GALLANTRY

BY THE TIME breakfast began, Peter seemed to be getting on famously with terrible Uncle Dan Thomas. He had no eye for Mary whatever, and presently she sat at the table, with her back stiff and her face expressionless, so deep was her disappointment in the newcomer. For he hung upon the words of Uncle Dan. No matter what the big man said, the younger was sure to applaud. If it was some brutal jest, he broke into agreeable roars of laughter; and if it were a bit of practical wisdom, Peter Quince seemed to enjoy it no less. When Uncle Dan pounded on the table in the excess of pleasure, Peter pounded likewise. They ripened into such mutual good humor that at length Uncle Dan took note of the gloomy expression of the girl.

"Look at her," he said to Peter, "like a thunder-cloud setting there. Enough to take away a man's appetite! Ain't she?"

He made this remark while sandwiching fat slices of bacon between layers of sweet "pone," then poised the huge morsel in his unclean fist.

"It's a girl's duty to be pleasant," said Peter.

"You got sense, boy," said the mountaineer. "I'll say you got a pile of good sense! You hear what he says, Mary?"

"I hear him," she answered disdainfully.

"Look at her sneer!" roared Uncle Dan, beating the table in his rage, so that the dishes jumped under the blows. "Look at her making a mock and a scorn of me, and me her own blood uncle!"

"What blood of yours runs in me?" cried Mary suddenly, whipping Peter with a glance of furious contempt for allowing such words to be used to her in his presence.

"Well, ain't I your father's wife's brother?"

"But not the brother of my mother."

"Bah!" grumbled Uncle Dan Thomas. "It sure makes me tired to hear your talk. The way I was raised, I seen that the women folks was always on hand to do their work and set the meals on the table and then shut up! And it appears to me like it was good sense at that. Eh, boy?"

"That sounds very reasonable," said Peter Quince.

Once more the glance of Mary flashed across him and withered him with a touch of fire.

"But this is what I got to put up with all the time," said Uncle Dan. "There ain't no gratitude in that girl. She talks right up all the time, and there ain't never no sympathy for the kind of a dog's life that I lead. Mary, go get some whisky. It makes me dry to talk about you— it sure does!"

Mary rose slowly, and her frown told Peter plainly enough that whisky was the great controlling force in the life of her uncle and in the entire household as well. She brought from behind the door a great three-gallon demi-john, which she only managed to tilt up with great trouble. Peter instinctively rose to help her, but Uncle Dan quelled that at once.

"You set right where you be," he said, raising his immense and grimy hand. "I've seen some of the ways that young men and old 'uns put themselves out for slips of girls. It's a outrage, I say. Ain't they able to help themselves? Yes, and to help others, too. And if they ain't, they ain't no good. They need disciplining—they need the whip, I say. Eh, boy?"

"I suppose you're right," said Peter.

But though he answered obediently enough, he had to look down to the floor for a moment before he dared trust himself to look into the face of the brute opposite him at the table.

"Put it away, boy!" commanded Uncle Dan. "Drink her down!"

And, so saying, he closed his eyes, leaned far back in his chair, and tilted at his lips half a glass of almost colorless home-made whisky, grinning with expectation of pleasure. But Peter, choosing the instant the eyes were fully closed, changed the direction of his own glass, as it was nearing his very lips, and hurled the contents through the open door. The result was that when Uncle Dan put down his glass, coughing, as the fiery stuff tore its way down to a settling place in his vitals, he found the glass of Peter empty before him, and the eyes of Peter unclouded with moisture.

The amazement of the mountaineer was beautiful to watch. His eyes started, his mouth gaped, and he beheld Peter with a species of horror. Twice he turned his glass between thumb and forefinger. Then he peered cautiously up to Peter's calm face again.

"What do you think of it?" he asked.

"Rather good," said Peter, "and rather mild."

"Mild!" breathed the other, who had been counting upon that acid stuff to send Peter gasping and coughing for water. "Well," he continued, "I see that you got the making of a man in you these days—got the makings of a real mountaineer in you. Eh, Mary?"

Mary could not speak. She was watching Peter Quince with utter astonishment, and perhaps the trick of the moonshine and its disappearance made her suspect for the first time that Peter was playing no more than a part with her uncle.

"Another drink, girl!" cried Uncle Dan. "And what of a few passes with the dice, Peter, my boy?"

He took a greasy and battered box from the shelf on the instant and spun the time-yellowed cubes across the surface of the table. It needed only a glance from Peter to make sure that the mountaineer was an expert cheat. He held the box with his thumb and his last two fingers; with the first two fingers he was ready to handle the dice as they left or entered the box, and all so swiftly that the eye could not follow him.

"What do we play for?" said Peter.

"Fun or money," said Uncle Dan. "It makes no difference to me. I'm your man for any kind of a game, high or low."

"Before I lose," said Peter, "what's the price of that gray horse in the corral?"

"There's no price on Bad Luck," put in the girl.

"Hell of fire!" thundered Uncle Dan. "Who asked you to put in your face, you—"

The heart of Peter Quince stopped beating; for, though he had many a time heard men quarrel with women, this was the first time he had ever heard a woman cursed, and it gave him a singularly hungry desire to take the fat throat of Uncle Dan in his hands and sink his thumbs into the hollow of the neck.

"Get out of the house!" bellowed Uncle Dan, as Mary disappeared. "As for the price of that there horse," said Uncle Dan, "there ain't another like him in the mountains, and that's flat!"

"And the price?"

"If he ain't worth five hundred, he's worth nothing."

"Well," said Peter, "that's not too much—if the horse is gentle. But I'm not much of a rider."

It seemed to him that the eyes of the other turned to fire. He ground his knuckles with a grating sound through the dense and brittle stubble of beard which tufted his chin, and he seemed to drink in Peter. Five hundred dollars—those bright eyes were saying in the silence. And for that sum, Peter could guess, a murder would be easily done in that house.

"Suppose I saddle him for you," said the mountaineer, "and then suppose that you try him out?"

"I wouldn't get on him," said Peter, "unless I could saddle him myself. I wouldn't trust myself for a minute on the back of a rough horse."

The sneer of Uncle Dan was half regret and half contempt.

"Curse such a man!" he growled, seeing his hopes diminish. Just what those hopes were, Peter could only guess; but he could take it for granted that Uncle Dan had been profoundly hoping that Bad Luck would so start the work of the destruction of Peter that he, Uncle Dan, would need to give only the finishing touches, and that the sum of five hundred dollars and more—which he must infer was with Peter—would be his for the taking. What, indeed, could be neater than this? But, since there was no hope of pushing the thing through, he shook his head.

"Then we'll sit here quiet and play our dice," he said. "The horse ain't so gentle after all. He's a wild one, but

I thought maybe you'd like to try out his tricks. He's got good ones!"

"Do you put the same price on a broken and an unbroken horse?" asked Peter.

"Ah, ah!" cried the mountaineer. "Is that all of it? You ride as well as the next man, but you want to beat my price down? Is that it?"

"I can sit in a saddle, that's all," said Peter.

Uncle Dan flamed into a rage.

"If you sit the saddle on Bad Luck for two minutes, he's your horse for nothing. D'ye understand? And the devil take you!"

"Very well. Where's a saddle for him?"

"Yonder. I'll throw in the saddle, if you ride him!"

"Very well," said Peter, "but I hate to take so many things from you!"

He took the saddle over the hook of his arm. As a matter of fact, he had not the slightest idea that he might be able to stay in the saddle on the stallion; but he felt that one hard fall would not break his neck unless the luck was against him. And, in the meantime, the stakes were large. Most of all there was that feeling of destiny still at work in him—that somehow and at some time the horse must surely become his! Why was this not the occasion?

He stepped outside the shack, and, as the cool of the morning bathed his temples, he realized for the first time how far he had been driven by loathing of the big mountaineer. But he went on down the hill toward the corral, where Bad Luck was kept, and as he went he talked with Uncle Dan, who was lumbering behind.

"How old is that horse?"

"Coming on five."

"Know his father?"

"Never seen him."

"His mother?"

"Never seen her."

That was the history of Bad Luck, as Peter received it. He reached the corral.

"Hey!" said Uncle Dan. "You didn't bring no rope to catch him!"

"I don't need one," said Peter. "Besides, I couldn't handle one if I had it."

His head was turned to Uncle Dan as he spoke, and he was sidling through the fence.

"Look out!" cried the mountaineer involuntarily.

Hoofs rushed from the farther side of the corral but Peter slipped on through the bars, and, as he rose, Bad Luck swerved sharply in his charge, raced around the inclosure, and came to a halt just before the stranger.

"It ain't possible! I ain't seeing right!" Peter heard Uncle Dan grumbling in the distance. But, in the meantime, the bridle had been slipped over the head of Bad Luck, and the horse was merely shaking his head and apparently amusing himself with the feel of the bit in his mouth, one ear pricked and one ear flattened. The saddle was raised. He whirled about to snort at it, then sniffed it, very like a dog, and, finally, he let Peter slide it upon his back, while Uncle Dan in the distance shouted with rage and astonishment.

"You've doped that horse!" he yelled at Peter.

But Peter returned no answer. Instead, he drew the cinches taut and swung into the saddle. There he waited. The body of the stallion was quivering beneath him and sinking a little until the coiled muscles would be ready for the spring; and Peter himself was shaken like a leaf in a shivering wind. He was frankly as frightened as though he sat that instant athwart a thunderbolt, ready to be launched into space. But when Bad Luck had fully crouched, he straightened again, turned his head about, and nibbled at the toe of Peter's shoe. Then he tossed his head and shook it, until the bridle jingled, and now he broke into a gentle trot. Straight up to the door of the cabin Peter guided him and there swung down to the ground again, while Uncle Dan was swinging up the hill, pouring out a melody of abuse. He was still storming and raging when he arrived.

"You've doped him!" thundered Uncle Dan. "Curse you, you've doped him! Gimme them reins and—"

"Listen to me," said Peter.

"You got no words that count with me."

"I have some heavy words, though," said Peter. "Listen to this, for instance!"

And snatching Uncle Dan's revolver, he fired into the air; a light clang of metal showed that he had struck a target.

"Is that your game?" thundered Uncle Dan Thomas. "Why, I'll turn you into a sieve!"

"Look yonder!" said Peter, and pointed.

He had indicated the top of the chimney which protruded above the roof, and on top of the chimney there was a conical cap which stood upon three legs, one of which was torn in two.

"Look close!" said Peter, and fired again; the conical cap sagged upon one leg only. "Again!" said Peter, and, as his gun spoke, the cap leaped from the chimney and sailed away into the air. Peter dropped the revolver into his holster.

"I'll have no more trouble with you," he said to Uncle Dan. "You'll just stand quiet from now on, eh?"

Uncle Dan was in fact transformed. He could only gape on his strange and youthful visitor.

"Call Mary," said Peter.

Uncle Dan obeyed.

"Louder!" said Peter.

"I'll take no orders from you!"

So Peter stepped to him and shoved the muzzle of the gun deep into the stomach of the mountaineer. "Now," he said, "talk soft and talk low when you hear me speak. I'd rather blow you in two than anything in the world. Call Mary!"

The voice of Uncle Dan rose in thunder, and Peter dropped the revolver back into the holster.

"If you think," he said, "that you can jump for cover before I can get this gun out of the holster, go ahead and try it. The grave digging won't be my work!"

But Uncle Dan was completely cowed. The drinking had been a little early in the morning even for him. Now he was left cold of blood and cold of spirit. Here Mary came out from among the trees. She needed only a glance to tell her that trouble was on foot.

"Mary," said Peter Quince, "are you happy here?"

"Oh, no!"

"What claim has he on you?"

"None in the world except this land which he took charge of."

"Is it his land?"

"Mary!" shouted Uncle Dan.

"Not unless he cheated Dad into giving it to him!"

"When we're alone—" began Uncle Dan.

"Why have you stayed with him?"

"Where else could I go? Besides, I was afraid to run away."

"Mary, will you saddle your horse and pack your clothes, while I keep an eye on this swine?"

"What do you mean, Peter?"

"To take you away."

"But where?"

"Anywhere you wish."

"But—"

"Are you afraid of me, Mary?"

"I'll go!" cried Mary.

"Are you crazy?" cried Uncle Dan. "You've never seen this man before, Mary!"

"Hush!" said Peter. "She knows more of me in one glance than she'd know of you in a thousand years. But be quiet, Uncle Dan. The more I see of you the more I think I should tie you to that tree, yonder, before we go, and let you work your way loose from the ropes, eh?"

The threat turned Uncle Dan Thomas white, and he had no more to say. But Mary had been electrified. Down the hill she raced, and presently Peter heard her singing from one of the corrals. She appeared again, galloping a stout roan up the slope. She threw the reins, as she reached the house, leaped from the saddle and was gone inside. In five minutes she came out again with a bundle tucked under her arm.

"Is that all you have, Mary?" asked Peter.

"Yes."

"If I had time," said Peter, "I'd like to talk to you with a horsewhip. That's the sort of conversation you'd understand, Uncle Dan. But we're too busy to stay. But, remember this: If you try to follow, I'll stop at the next town and tell them the truth of how you've treated Mary. They'll give you all the law you want and something more, Uncle Dan. Keep that smoking in your pipe—and good-bye!"

For Mary was now in the saddle, and in another instant they were clattering down the trail as fast as their horses could gallop; for they must get out of range before Uncle Dan could run into the house, snatch a gun and come out again. They succeeded so well that not a shot echoed behind them.

6. UNDER THE STARS

But the joy of the adventure, the excitement of the possible chase and even the pretty face of Mary beside him, were very little to Peter. He was rapt in the contemplation of the speed and the silken-smooth paces of the gray stallion. For Bad Luck ran like the wind, as swiftly and as easily. He danced down the ragged and steep trail lightly, and he floated up the valley. At the crest beyond, where they drew rein to survey the situation and the thing they had done, Bad Luck was hardly breathing, and the roan was half blown.

"But now, if I go back—" began Mary.

"Why should you go back?"

"But where can I go, Peter?"

"Why not anywhere?"

"I have no other home."

"You've no relatives?"

"Only my mother's sister in Kinsey City."

"But why not go to her?"

"How shall I know that I'd be welcome?"

"There's no man or woman in the world that wouldn't make you welcome, Mary."

"Peter, why do you say such things?"

"Because they're true."

"Hush, Peter!"

"If I had a mirror, Mary, I'd show you a picture that would convince you."

"Peter, you're only trying to make me blush."

"Then I'm having wonderful luck. It's almost as if—"

"What?"

"Mary," he broke in upon himself, "how many young men have you known?"

"In the last four years—just none!"

"Then no one has told you a number of things about yourself."

"Such as what, Peter?"

"When we find a finer hilltop, I'll try to tell you, Mary."

And at that, as though she guessed what he had meant for the first time, she started the roan ahead, and Peter drifted behind her with Bad Luck. He could not help feeling that he had her as completely in his hand as the speed of Bad Luck commanded that of the roan. Even as she hurried the roan along now, with her head leaned forward resolutely, he was confident that a single word would make her turn and laugh back at him with happy eyes. And Peter rejoiced in his strength!

He was deciding many things about girls in general, as he galloped along. It was all the manner in which one approached them, he concluded. Here, at a single meeting, he had won the confidence of Mary. Yet, had he talked to her as he talked to that first Mary, he could not doubt that he would have failed. But each girl was like a different musical instrument; they must be played in a unique fashion. And Peter felt in himself a limitless ability to discover ways and means.

Perhaps it proved, more than anything else, that Peter was very young, and that all young men are a little arrogant. But at least he was vowing, as he cantered along, that he would take the best care of Mary. From pity he passed to a tenderer feeling; a haze of gentle sadness held him so rapt that he was amazed.

At midday they had a lunch of roasted squirrels, whose heads had been nipped off by bullets from the revolver of Uncle Dan Thomas in the expert hand of Peter Quince.

"But what will we do when Uncle Dan overtakes us?" cried Mary, trembling, as the dark thought struck her. "What will we do when we are arrested for stealing—"

"Uncle Dan will never bother you again," said Peter. "I think I know that."

"Are you sure?"

"The story we could tell about him would shame him ut of the country."

For all his pretended surety, his glance was ever for the ail behind them during that day, but in the evening they eached a village on the little branch railroad which ould carry them to Kinsey City; and, as they rode own its street, through the bars of light which poured out f unshaded windows and through open doors, he relaxed is vigilance and began to feel that the game was already on. They registered on the stained sheet of the book in he little hotel, and Peter saw her write the name Mary In- ram; and she in turn saw him write Peter Quince.

"And, I s'pose," said the clerk, "that you'll want next- oor rooms, so's you can talk through the wall?"

Peter glanced at the girl to see how she bore that sally, nd he was delighted to find that, though she had colored little, she was looking steadfastly at the clerk, as though, a fact, he had not been there.

"You may stop your supposing," said Peter with dignity, nd the clerk shrank into a smaller compass.

Neither did Mary speak of the matter again, as they sat t the table in the dining room of the hotel; but there as a quiet and possessive tenderness in her eyes, now nd again, as she looked at Peter. And sometimes she rew rosy with confusion when nothing at all had been aid. Peter thought her charming, far more charming than ver before; and when supper was ended he took her out or a walk, as though both of them were not numbed with eariness from the long ride and the excitement of that ay! But if their bodies failed them, their hearts did not; nd though their feet stumbled through the alkali dust, eir eyes were wandering among the stars. Beyond the dge of the village they reached a knoll, with a circlet f trees and a soft, warm wind whispering through them.

There, Mary stopped, and Peter, brushing against her, topped also. A trembling pulse of excited happiness was hrobbing in him, higher and higher every instant.

"Oh, Peter Quince," she whispered at last, "I—I—I ink that's a perfect name for you."

"Why, Mary?"

"Because it's a different name, and you're different om other people."

"How different, Mary?"

"Because I'm sure that any other man would have kissed me long ago."

He caught at her, but she dodged away with wonderful swiftness and was gone. Peter wanted to follow her. With all his heart he yearned to pursue. But a great, strong instinct told him to sit quietly upon a rock and not stir. He obeyed the instinct, while Mary hovered in the near distance, a slender shadow, and half-guessed-at features under the starlight.

"I wish I could follow you," he said.

"No, no," said Mary, with a touch of what might be pique or disgust in her voice. "I know you're much too dignified for that, Peter!"

"But suppose that I followed you and—frightened you Mary?"

She came suddenly back to him, just as that profound instinct had told him she would come.

"Peter Quince," she cried to him, "what a heart of gold you have!"

And so, how he could not quite tell, she was in his arms—he had kissed her, and the sound of her breathing was like the soft, warm wind in the aspens above them.

"But who in all the world could I trust," she was saying, "if not you, Peter, dear?"

And what was the thought in the strange mind of Peter? Was it a tender ecstasy? No; for he was registering this conclusion in his heart of hearts: "Never follow a girl, for she will come back to you." But he said aloud: "When I saw you this morning, it seemed to me that my life began—that this is the first day I have really lived!"

"And when I saw those straight blue eyes of yours, Peter, I knew that the sad time had ended for me. Peter dear, it seems to me that there was never a time when I didn't love you!"

They went slowly, slowly back toward the hotel, passing behind the line of houses.

"I have no money," he said. "Are you afraid of that?"

"Of course not! We're young and strong. That's our wealth, dear!"

Loud voices poured out to them through an open window. They could not help but look inside, and there they saw a middle-aged couple in a hot debate. The man stood in the middle of the room, beating one hand into the palm of the other to make his points, and she was pitching sharply back and forth in a rocking-chair, pretending to sew, but stabbing blindly at the cloth, her thin lips compressed in a straightening line.

"Doggone me if I ain't tired of it!" roared the husband. "Here I go working my hands to the bone every day, all day, and when I come home there ain't never no smile for me; there ain't nothing but nagging—why ain't I making more money—why ain't I saving more—when are we going to get a piano for Anne?"

"I don't expect you to talk reasonable any more," broke in the wife. "You talk like I was asking things for myself. I ain't. I'm asking them for your own flesh and blood— your own daughter. Ain't she to have a chance in life?"

"She's got as good a chance as the next one."

"You got no thought of nothing but your own comfort —your own soft bed and your own full stomach."

Mary drew at the arm of Peter and tugged him along.

"That terrible woman!" she whispered. "Let's not stay to hear her raging!"

"Why is she afraid to listen?" thought Peter to himself, as he walked on with her, holding her close all the while. "Books say that women are curious, and from all that I have seen of them, curious they are indeed! And yet she will not stay to see this and hear it? Then it must be that she did not wish me to hear it. And she did not wish me to hear it, because in that way I might come to think ill of marriage. That must be it! She's clever then and capable of being secret!"

Such were the thoughts of Peter, as they moved on; and, though Mary was talking all the while, he only heard her with half an ear. She was telling him that their life together should come to no such a halting place as the one which they had just looked in upon. Their love would outlast their lives, and to the end there would be only tenderness for one another. So they went on until he had brought her to her door in the hotel, but here, having cast a glance up and down the hall to make sure that they could not be spied upon, she suddenly clung to him with her face lifted and a sort of desperation in her eyes.

"Oh, Peter, Peter, Peter!" she cried softly. "If I leave you now I'm afraid that I'll never see you in the morning. It seems that more than one glorious day with you would be more than I could be granted. And I have a nightmare feeling that I shall never again see the sunshine in your yellow hair, Peter, or see your eyes laughing at me."

He drew her very close with cherishing hands. It made him feel like a man of middle age to have this burden placed in his care.

"Mary dear," whispered Peter, "you will see that I have a long life to love you and will be near you every day."

"But look at me—look at me!"

She took his face between her hands and made him confront the light. She studied him through a long moment of silence, with an expression half enraptured and half despairing; then she loosed him with a sigh and slipped inside her door. He tried to follow, to draw out a fuller explanation from her. But the key clicked in the lock. He called to her in a whisper, but after a time he heard a muffled sobbing and knew that she must have flung herself face downward on the bed, crying.

Truly they were very strange creatures, these women. Here she was weeping her heart out at the very instant when he had confessed his love for her, and she had told her love for him! It would be pleasant to say that he was made grave and humble by this glimpse of the depth of her emotion. But this is a true history of Peter Quince and not a romance. As a matter of fact, Peter was not a little gratified to think that he had stirred her so greatly. It was like a taste of wine to a giddy brain. He had to have someone to talk to—to confide in—and, since he knew no one in that town, he very naturally went down the stairs and found his horse in the corral behind the barn. There was no other animal in the little enclosure with the stallion; he was neither eating nor lying down after his hard day of travel, but, with his head lifted and his mane blown, with a starshine glistening along his silken flanks and a posture like a sculpture in marble, he was staring out over the corral bars—at what?

Some of the delight slipped out of the body of Peter Quince and out of his heart. Then, from far away, a coyote called. The stallion stirred a pace to the side. Again

he coyote's cry wavered thin and small across the darkness, and the face of Mary went out from the mind's
eye of Peter Quince. He walked directly up in front of
the gray horse, but, though he spoke, the stallion remained with the high head, facing north into the wind,
north into the coyote's cry. Peter turned squarely about
and faced in the same direction. Before him the mountains tossed indistinct and ragged heads against the stars,
and the stars themselves winked blue and small, and the
cold, pure fragrance of the pines was in the breeze.

It was a night of great charm.

It meant to Peter more than he could put into words.
But one thing at least he knew, that he could not marry
Mary, nor any other woman, until he met one with all the
strength, the purity, the mystery of that mountain night.
He knew, too, that something had been born into his
blood with his birth which gave him a right and a claim
to life as free as the wild life of that coyote which was
calling far away among the mountains. He knew for the
first time that his lonely youth, cut away from the com-
panionship of other boys, had not been a pure affectation.
Yes, he was different, and the others had felt the difference
even more than he.

The coyote's cry died out in the distance, and Bad Luck
dropped his soft muzzle on the shoulder of the master.
And the hand of the master went up around the head of
the horse. It seemed to Peter that all his happiness with
Mary had been nothing compared with this, for Bad Luck
understood, and what woman in all the world ever could
do as much?

7. FROM BEHIND A COPSE

PETER WAS twenty-four hours on the other side of eighteen, and at eighteen young men do not hesitate very long.
What Peter did was to go straight back to his room in the
hotel and write a letter.

Mary dear: What I want most is to make you happy, and I can see now that you are right. The best way for me to make you happy is never to see you again. I am not the kind of man who can marry and settle down. And, therefore, I can't give you a contented life.

I'm enclosing with this enough money to pay your fare to Kinsey City. There I know that you'll find the right man for you. Good luck to him and great happiness to you.

Peter Quince.

He reread the letter, decided that it was all he could say, and then went out and slipped the missive under her door. When he straightened he was aware of a great shadow looming in the darkness of the hallway, and even in that obscure light he could make out the jagged features of Uncle Dan Thomas. He had time for that and nothing more, for a long line of dull light showed the barrel of a revolver pointed at him.

"Kid," muttered Uncle Dan, "you've made a good play. Now, march downstairs ahead of me. I got a pile to say to you and little time to say it in."

Peter, perforce, obeyed. He walked calmly enough down the stairs and, according to directions, left the hotel by the side entrance and stood under the stars once more. He was terribly frightened, but he was too busy thinking to give himself much time for fear to take hold of his mind.

"Now, son," said the older man, "I ain't going to ask you to hold up your hands. I ain't going to search you for my gun that you stole. I'm just going to shoot you dead if you stir a hand. What I want to know first is, what have you done with Bad Luck?"

"He's in the little corral behind the barn."

"That's straight, because I seen him there. And what have you done with Mary?"

"She's in the room next to mine upstairs."

"I guess that's true, too. Where's she bound for?"

"Kinsey City."

"With you?"

"Alone."

"Well," said Uncle Dan, "she'll go straight back home with me. Who'd I have to cook my chuck if I lost her? But first I got to get through with you."

"What are you going to do with me?" asked Peter.

"This!" said the mountaineer, and with his left hand he shook out the noose of a lariat.

"Hard luck," said Peter, and, as he spoke, he struck. Ordinarily he would have been shot dead, even as his hand started to move; but his victim had been so docile, and the mind of the mountaineer was so full of his revenge that he was caught unprepared. A hand which had gained weight from constant play with a burly sledgehammer delivered a hook in such perfect style that the heart of the old one-legged man would have burst with pride. A well delivered hook has several features about it. It begins at the hip or lower. It shoots high, skims over the shoulder of the opponent, curls in and at the last instant of impact, cracks downward. It is both a twist and a jar at once. And when this blow landed accurately on the point of Uncle Dan's chin, he did not fall backward with its weight; instead, he crumpled forward upon his face, with a numbed brain.

Peter disentangled his feet from the arms which had fallen loosely about them. Then he picked up Uncle Dan's gun and dropped it into his coat pocket. Then he sat down upon a neighboring stump and waited for Dan Thomas to wake up. This occurred presently with a prodigious groan and yawn. Uncle Dan sat up and glowered bewilderingly at the youth.

"Listen to me," said Peter.

"Where's your friend?" gasped Uncle Dan. "Where's the dirty sneak that soaked me from behind?"

"Here," said Peter. "Want to smell him?" And he thrust out his hard right fist. Uncle Dan was silenced for the first time in his life.

"I've seen your face, and I've seen your work," said Peter Quince, "and I don't like either! If I were not a soft-hearted fool, I'd crack your skull with the butt of your own gun and let them bury you in the morning. But I think you have brains enough to soak up one lesson. If you need another later on, I'll come to give it to you. I'm going to be in touch with Mary. If I hear that you've

come near her, so much as written to her, I'm going to
come back for you. I'm going to hunt you down. I'm
going to kill you, Uncle Dan. D'you hear?"

He leaned forward as he spoke, and terrible Uncle
Dan Thomas shrank away from him.

"If you so much as cast an eye on her," went on Peter
Quince, with the same unhurried enunciation, "I'll travel
halfway around the world to find you. And when I find
you, there'll be an end of you. I'll lay you out with your
face to the sky to wait for the buzzards."

With this, Peter Quince rose, stretched himself carefully
and was about to turn away, when a second thought came
to him. He drew from his coat pocket the revolver which
he had so recently taken away from Uncle Dan Thomas
and dropped it on the ground beside the latter.

"In the meantime," he said, "if you get in trouble you
may need this gun."

And so saying, he deliberately turned his back upon
the fallen man and strolled to the hotel side entrance.
Thrice Uncle Dan Thomas raised the revolver and sighted
carefully at the leisurely figure, and thrice it seemed to
him that a leaden weight bore his hand down. He had no
chance of missing the shot at such a short distance, and
yet he felt strangely certain that the youth was watching
him every instant, with a sort of extra sense, and that the
instant he pulled the trigger Peter Quince would dodge
away and then come leaping back at him with death in
his hand.

So Uncle Dan did not shoot. Instead, he waited until
some of the ache had left his brain, and then he rose
unsteadily to his feet. He made off through the darkness
like a drunken man, shambling and stumbling over every
projecting root, for he knew himself for the first time in
his life, and that self was not the hero he had always believed, but a miserable, cowardly soul wrapped up in the
body of a big man.

As for Peter Quince, when he reached his room he did
not sit for a long time in the dark, thinking of all that
had passed. He did not worry and ponder about the future and the happiness of Mary. No; instead of doing any
of these things which book heroes would have done, Peter
went straight to bed and slept, like one stunned with

fatigue, for a full five hours. Then he wakened, still drunk
with sleep, dressed, went down the stairs and to the corral,
where he saddled the stallion and rode Bad Luck out of
town. He came back, however, when the business day
might be said to have begun, and asked at the station for
the time when the first train started for Kinsey City. It was
a scant hour away, so Peter drew his horse back into a
little copse near the station and waited.

He did not have to wait the full hour. Before half that
time elapsed, Mary Ingram came, and she did not come
alone! Oh, faith of womankind! At her side walked a
stalwart youth, with her parcel of belongings under his
arm and a joyous air of mastery and possession in his
face. He walked like the emperor of the world, and up
to him Mary was looking as meek and as mild and as
untroubled as a lamb beside the bellwether!

Peter could not believe his eyes. He looked, and he
looked again. For where was the wan and shrinking creature whom he was to pity, and the sight of whom was to
tug at his heartstrings? And where was the true philos-
ophy in his heart? His controlling impulse was to rush out
and break the tall youth into many small portions. But
then he realized that he would be making himself ridiculous. Besides, he swore to himself that he did not care
—that he merely despised Mary. For a whole half hour,
nevertheless, he remained in the covert, staring out at her
and torturing himself with her pretty face. And at last the
train thundered out of the distance, came crashing and
panting to a stop, making the ground still quiver with its
breathings, as it stood still; and now Mary was taken
aboard by the cavalier. So great was his courtesy that he
went inside with her and found her a seat on the shady
side of the coach. All this Peter Quince could make sure
of by standing on tiptoe in his stirrups. Nay, still more,
the gallant fellow was actually sitting down beside her and
making gay conversation until such time as the train should
start.

But Mary was laughing only feebly at his jokes. For the
major part, she was dwelling on his face with that lamb-
like look of devotion which was so familiar to Peter
Quince. Suddenly the train began to move. Now for a
wild scamper on the part of the cavalier. But no, he did

not stir! There he sat ensconced at the side of Mary Ingram, while the train pulled out from the station, and his arm passed round the shoulders of the girl, just as though they were alone in that coach. And he was pointing out through the window to some feature of the landscape, and his manner was that of a man who owns the mountain toward which he is pointing.

So they passed forever out of the view of Peter. What did Peter do? He neither blushed for shame nor cursed for fury, but, tilting back his head, he broke into a gay, loud laughter which startled some people walking past near his covert. Then he twisted Bad Luck around and galloped away from the town.

He did his best thinking while he rode, and what he concluded was something as follows: That a man may think that a girl has fallen in love with him, but, as a matter of fact, she had simply fallen in love with the first man who happens along—she had fallen in love with mankind, one might say. And so it was with Mary Ingram. The time had come for her to love; she had taken Peter as the first man, and, when he passed on, she had taken number two with equal pleasure.

"And yet," said Peter Quince, "no other man but I saw the bud open to the flower; and it was I who breathed the first perfume. No matter how many men pass through her life, she must see my face drifting between their eyes and hers."

Such was the conclusion of Peter, but, as a matter of fact, he only half believed it. How much vital conceit was taken out of him by that adventure one could hardly estimate.

8. A FIGHTING PHILANDERER

FOR FOUR YEARS after that Peter wandered here and there, trying to make out that he was a useful and industrious member of society, but knowing very well all the time that he was nothing of the kind. He tried to be a miner, and a miner he was, off and on and here and there, but though he loved to ramble across the mountains on a quest which could actually have no ending, because it was more than mere metal he hunted, yet, when it came to the actual labor of breaking ground, that was quite another matter. He detested it with all his soul. He worked a year and a half, and at the end of that time he was known as the worst prospector who ever looked at the world between a burro's ears.

Cowpunching was little better. He became a marvelous rider, and he worked with a rope until he was an ambidextrous expert. To break a horse was a pleasant and easy game for Peter, and to rope a cow in quick time was equally pleasant. But for the long, long, monotonous grind which makes up the daily work of a cowpuncher he had no liking. To ride fence drove him mad. Half a day of it made him quit any job. And for building tanks, or dragging bogged cows out of the mud of them, he had little greater liking. Therefore, he made the worst of cowpunchers.

To those who saw him during round-up time, when he was a brilliant figure, or to those who saw him breaking horses in the spring of the year, it seemed that he must be a star among the stars, yet it was known that he was never retained for more than three months at the most. Naturally, since he could not keep up with his regular and honest work, he tried his luck at cards; but, since he could not induce himself to follow sharp practices, he lost at cards what little he won at work.

So the four years passed and left some calluses on the hands of Peter Quince and turned his hair a darker and more coppery gold and faded the blue of his eyes to a colder color and set a deep vertical wrinkle between his eyes and carved his features a little more sharply. He had more muscles and stronger ones. And his body was crossed and spotted with scars. For, alas, that we should have to say it, our Peter Quince was a fighter born and bred!

It would be pleasant if we could say that Peter fought a great many times simply because he was often cornered, and because bold and overbearing men strove to take advantage of this golden-haired and handsome youth. It would be pleasant to say this, but it would be far indeed from the truth; for, though Peter was as handsome as an angel, when he was angered he was more like a destroying angel than any other, and men would as soon have laid hands upon him as other dogs will set teeth in a bull terrier.

But the ugly truth is that Peter loved fighting, and he loved it for its own sake. He would do anything and go anywhere for the sake of a fight. He would battle with knives or guns or fists or rough and tumble, which is the most terrifying form of all combat. He found big men and strove eagerly to bring them to a battle in which he might be the opponent. He coaxed men up to the line. He pretended cowardice and fear to encourage the others to such a point that shame would make them go on.

Neither was Peter always successful. Once a big Swede, who had been a champion wrestler, got him with a strangle hold and all but killed him. Peter recovered his wind, became the Swede's friend and admirer long enough to learn all he knew of wrestling, and then he trounced the Swede publicly with his own tricks. This was not romantic or generous; it was simply Peter Quince.

Another time Peter ran afoul of an Italian who shunned all weapons saving knives. Before Peter could turn about, two long and narrow-bladed knives were buried in his anatomy. Afterward, he lay in bed for three months, rose, found the Italian, and by dint of flattery garnered from the fellow what he knew of knife play. It was not hard for Peter to learn these things. He had the instinct for destruction, muscles of India rubber and nerves of steel. The result was that he picked up such valuable information lightning fast. He learned how to throw a knife with a flip of the wrist from the palm, or by spinning it out of thumb and forefinger.

Afterward, for that was Peter's way, he picked a quarrel with his teacher. It was not that he wanted revenge, or that he was ungrateful. But he simply felt that there was no other way to test his newly acquired skill. They fought, and the Italian did not die from his wounds, but it kept Peter busy for six months paying the hospital bills.

He had other unfortunate accidents. For instance, a giant Negro once grew excited and hurled at Peter a great armchair which went through a window and carried Peter along with it. Peter was cut to pieces with the flying glass. When he recovered he found the Negro, though the trail carried him to New Orleans and back again. He left that colored gentleman to be buried by charity and went blithely on his way.

There were gun fights, also, but not very many of these after his nineteenth year, for it was at that time that he met the famous Jim Crawley and killed him in a fair duel, with a whole town looking on from behind windows. The spectators scattered abroad more, or less and told what they knew, and the result was that men shunned conflict with Peter Quince, as far as guns were concerned. And his greatest art of all was left undeveloped. He practiced it religiously, sadly, every day, feeling all the while that the time would never come when he could use it. In the meantime, he picked up what other crumbs of battle came his way.

It is little wonder that in the eyes of sheriffs he was an unlovely character. It is still smaller doubt that he was less popular among the mothers who had daughters of a marriageable age than he was with the sheriffs. For Peter was beginning to be well known as a philanderer.

Still the power of a name or the power of chance made it always a Mary. There were other affairs, to be sure, but the Marys were the important ones. The third Mary he found in Montana, a Norwegian girl with corn-colored hair and a skin that looked perishable to the touch and a disposition like a blessed saint dwelling in another world. Peter made wild love to her for three days, believed himself happy for a week, and then remembered a story of a gold ledge which he had heard from the lips of a dying prospector a year before.

He went south, prospected furiously for a month, forgot all about Mary, and then he was visited in his camp by three big blond men who sat blandly beside his fire and told him that they had come to take him back to their sister. Peter Quince lighted a cigarette and beamed tenderly upon them. They were all big men. Any one of them was capable of doing enough fighting to afford him pleasure for a day. But here they were offering themselves as a sacrifice all at one time, as a sort of hecatomb, one might say. So Peter rose and smote the nearest one upon the root of the jaw. Then he dived at the knees of a second and found himself involved with two hundred pounds of hard muscle and stout bone and the heart of a lion. But Peter himself fought like a raw edge of lightning. He sent one sprawling and then dropped the third. Whereupon all three rose from the ground again and came at him in a mass.

It was a gorgeous fight. And when at last one man lay prone with a broken jaw, and the two eyes of another were swelled shut, and the shoulder of another was so bruised by a fall that he could not lift his arm, Peter sat down on the fellow's back and swore to the tender face of the moon that it was the happiest evening of his life!

That was the end of Mary number three. The fourth Mary came from Boston, visited at her father's ranch, saw Peter in the offing and vowed that a figure from an Italian painting had started into life and left the canvas. A day later she danced with Peter at a country dance, and that finished affairs. She threw caution to the winds. For half a month they were happy, while the countryside buzzed with the chatter about this romance. And then Peter grew restless, for the lady from Boston was starting to plan his future, which began, of course, with a special course in a university, preferably Harvard. This was not all. The school of culture must be entered and graduated from. Life, it seemed, was tremendously complex.

"But," said Peter one day, "how could you ever have looked at me, or listened to such a boor, Mary?"

"Oh," said Mary, "of course a girl is different."

"Well," said Peter, "when we go East I'll have to spend most of my time with the girls then."

"Peter!" she cried.

"Well?" said he.

"What a terrible thing to say!"

"What a comfortable thing," replied Peter.

This was how the first quarrel started. There was no time for a second. Peter recalled a certain blue-hearted lake between two snow-sided mountains and off for that lake he started to fish and hunt to his heart's delight and let the shadow of the university and the Eastern culture disappear from his mind.

The fifth Mary came from Ireland, or at least she was rich in Irish blood. Peter was the guide of the hunting party of which she was one, but he forgot the pursuit of the big game in the pursuit of lovely Mary. Whether she was actually in love with him or simply weary of the stupid climbing, Peter could never be sure, but one white night, with a moon in the center of the sky, they eloped and fled back toward civilization.

They did not go to the nearest town, however, and before they arrived, the telegraph had cut in ahead of them, and the police were waiting for Peter. That evening he broke out of jail, climbed the wall of the hotel to Mary's room, and told her good-bye through the window. They vowed eternal faith and love, which Peter forgot in the curling smoke of his next cigarette, and Mary Norris married before the summer was out.

The sixth Mary, however, brought serious trouble upon Peter Quince. Be it remembered that by this time Peter was twenty-two, and by certain lights he looked a full five years older. He could no longer be taken as simply a romantic boy, yet nothing could have been more romantically foolish than the way he followed up his acquaintanceship with this sixth Mary. She was betrothed to a fine young fellow who had in expectation more millions of cash than Peter Quince could expect years of life. They had come West for a visit to a rough cousin in a rough country, and there they met dangerous Peter Quince.

On the first day he taught young Joseph Paul how to master a revolver for quick work. On the second day he taught Mary how to ride terrible Bad Luck. On the third day he was still teaching Mary. On the fourth day it was necessary for him to ride far off with her to pursue the lessons.

When she came back that night she told Joseph Paul that she no longer loved him, and when he asked her why, she very frankly told him that Peter Quince had set her heart on fire. So Joseph Paul went apart and thought matters over. The father of Peter Quince was John Quincy, a great outlaw. The father of Joseph Paul was Samuel Paul, a great baron of Wall Street. Where John Quincy had killed his man, Samuel Paul had crushed a thousand bank accounts. So that both of the young fellows came of fighting stock.

On this occasion it seemed wise to Joseph Paul to hire the work done. He bought the services of four hardy brigands and sent them at Peter, while he followed in the rear to make sure of the good work being completed. The four spilt upon Peter in the dark of night, like rain on the crest of a house. And Peter shot down the four without killing any, so greatly did luck favor him. But the fifth man who charged him he shot squarely through the heart, and that man was Joseph Paul.

Had Joseph been the son of a common man, all would have been well enough. The circumstances proved beyond the shadow of a doubt that Peter Quince had been assailed, and that he had merely fought to defend his person. But since Joseph was the son of a millionaire it became necessary to call the slayer a murderer. This was the epithet attached to Peter Quince at once. He was arrested and thrown into jail. And here to visit him came Mary Ringdon and stood trembling outside the bars of his cell.

"Peter, Peter!" she cried softly to him. "What can we do to save you? Mr. Paul's lawyers know that you'll be acquitted if you're tried. So they're working up mob spirit through the town, and before midnight the mob will storm the jail and take you out to——"

She had told Peter enough to convince him that it would not be wise to await the process of the law. He dug through a wall of the jail that night, made his way back to the stall of the stable in which Bad Luck was kept and fled south.

By that act he made himself an outlaw. He wound in a loose course, sometimes east and sometimes west, but bearing south eventually. Five famous men went out to stop him, as he headed toward their territory, and each made a greater and greater effort; for, as he traveled, the reward upon his head increased. Telegraph service spread the news across the country that the criminal was fleeing for the border more than a thousand miles away. Towns, counties, cities, which lay in or near his probable line of march, offered purses to be permanently added to the re-

ward upon his head, and every day greater bands of glory
and gold hunters prepared to block him away from his
safety.

Buck Jerome struck at him in Idaho. He rode a hundred miles in a single day, cast a wide loop around "Buck"
Jerome, and then raided Buck's own town and plundered
Buck's own house. He took only a few sacks of tobacco,
but he made a commotion and left a note to tell the
sheriff that he had been there. The shame was spoken of
for months afterward. Half of Buck's great reputation was
snuffed out at once.

In the meantime, the fugitive was drifting down into
Nevada. The reward offered for his apprehension, dead or
alive, had now climbed to twenty thousand dollars, a huge
sum to rest on a single head. Jeff Bertrand made the
most determined effort to hunt him down, as he crossed
the sagebrush state, but he doubled through Jeff's force
and headed on south and farther south, at such a rate
that no horse or series of horses could stay with him.
For Bad Luck seemed to thrive on hard running. He could
jog along all day and at the end of it have spirit and
strength enough to sprint away from a new pursuer.

Peter reached the western edge of Colorado with thirty
thousand dollars offered for his body. There he met the
famous Lew Maxwell, who had killed seven men as an
outlaw, and fourteen more as an officer of the law. But
Peter Quince was not his twenty-second victim, for Peter
split his thigh bone with one bullet and his right shoulder
with another and rode on with a fifty-thousand-dollar reward on his back the very next day, for Denver had
received the news and had opened her deep pockets to
aid the cause of justice.

But Bad Luck was growing thin, so Peter cached his
horse in a pleasant little nook where the grass was thick
and long. He spent two weeks resting himself and his
horse. Then, as rumors of his presence began to stir, he
was southward on the wing again.

Old Sheriff Al Foote went out with all his hundred men
to stop his passage through a corner of New Mexico. The
total result of that encounter was that five of the sheriff's
men were winged—none fatally, however—and Peter

Quince cantered on into Texas. It was said now that a hundred thousand dollars would be paid to the man who captured him. And there was hardly a boy past ten in Texas who did not polish up his old gun and ride out to take his luck of crossing the trail of the hunted man.

Yet Peter sifted through them. He managed it partly, no doubt, through tremendous luck, but it was partly through wonderful audacity. He had the appalling coolness of nerve to ride through the town of Inchley at high noon, watering his horse in the trough in front of the hotel-general merchandise store.

"What's your name?" called out an excited rancher, seeing at the watering trough a man who so closely answered the description of the famous outlaw.

"Name's Peter Quince!" laughed Peter.

The rancher hesitated and then laughed in turn. Of course, it was absurd that the outlaw should have ventured into the middle of a town at noon, where a hundred guns might bring him down. It simply happened that this fellow on the gray horse faintly resembled the famous Quince.

It was not until Peter had ridden on that the rancher understood that the absurdity was actually the truth. Then he leaped to his feet with an Indian yell which would have done credit to a Comanche. In twenty seconds as many men were in the saddle, but when they reached the bridge across the creek they found it in flames, and Peter was dipping out of sight beyond the next hill.

In their fury, they went back and held a meeting and raised five thousand dollars to add to the reward offered for the capture of Peter. But Peter was breezing on south and toward the Rio Grande, and the great "Lefty" Wautross was heading the organization of hunters who strove to bag him. All of Lefty's men could not touch him. But Lefty himself did. The next day they carried Lefty tenderly back to town, with Lefty praying, instead of groaning.

"Oh, Lord," murmured Lefty, "don't let nobody else capture him. Lemme have another chance at him, fair and square, before they get him behind the bars!"

The prayer of Lefty was answered. That same evening a horse plunged with its rider into the northern edge of the

Rio Grande, a dust-and-sweat-blackened horse and a dust-and-sweat-blackened man. They climbed out on the other side, renewed. The horse was a gray, and the man was Peter Quince.

9. THE GHOSTLY WALKER

THERE ARE very few men who can say that they are actually worth to themselves or to any other person more than a hundred thousand dollars; but Peter Quince could boast that the bullet which brought him down would mean a small fortune to the lucky fellow who fired. From a hundred to a hundred and twenty-five thousand dollars in cash was offered by more than a thousand individuals, towns, cities, counties and states—by newspapers and other corporations—and all because of that spectacular ride through five states by a solitary man, when all the police and the individual efforts in the West could not avail to stop him.

But, nevertheless, though he might be worth a hundred and twenty-five thousand dollars to someone else, he was not worth a penny to himself. He rode into the first Mexican town he reached and in bad Spanish offered to race Bad Luck against the pride of the town. Bad Luck was lean as a rail from long work. His hips and his ribs stuck out against his skin. His neck was a mere mass of sinews. So the Mexicans gladly accepted the challenge. By betting his horse, his clothes, his rifle and his revolver against odds, Peter Quince cleaned up some two hundred dollars in strange currency, when Bad Luck romped in a half dozen lengths ahead of the nearest pony, and Peter jogged calmly back to the hostelry.

It was the evening. Somewhere a bell was ringing among the hills on the edge of the town. The smell of cookery was in the air, cookery strange to the nostrils of Peter Quince. In the street there was a scurry of squealing dogs and pigs and children, which raised dust clouds that did not melt until they had out-topped the houses; but, in spite of that clamor of shrill voices, Peter lifted his head and was aware of the great peace of the night coming darkly across the sky. With all the noise it seemed to him more peaceful than anything he had ever known, and the firelight which began to play inside the doorways—yellow firelight against the whitewashed walls and the blue of the shadows—was all a part of the welcome for him.

He took Bad Luck to the stable and bedded him down with the greatest care. A bare-legged boy, with a thatch of black hair streaming down his forehead and his eyes glittering through the brush, stood by and marveled at the care he gave the poor brute.

"Ah, señor," he said at last, "is it the horse of the father of the girl you love?"

Peter laughed and gave him a silver coin. He did not know its denomination.

"Look!" he said, and, picking the child up under his arms, he swung him into the box stall.

The stallion swung with a squeal of rage and lunged at the urchin. But Peter drew him back in time and met the rush of Bad Luck with a word that quieted him.

"That," he said to the boy, "is why I take good care of my horse."

The child made no answer. He scurried to his mother, who worked in the kitchen of the hostelry, and there he told her that the newest guest of the tavern, the gringo with the gray horse, who had won the race and all the money, was no other than an enchanter who could talk with his horse in language which the brute understood as well as if it had been a man. To this tale the mother listened with a grunt which might have meant almost anything. For her part she did not care who or what the gringo was, as long as he paid double prices for everything, from the water and red fire called soup, which began his meal, to the wretched, lukewarm beer which ended it. But the stomach of the gringo seemed as strong as the black hoofs of his horse. He devoured his rations, shrugged his shoulders, lighted a cigarette, and strolled out to view the landscape and the town and the inhabitants thereof.

He was already known by the winning of the race, of course, and when he sauntered down the street bareheaded, with his blue eyes flashing here and there, and his golden hair shimmering in the chance rays of light which slid out through doors and windows, a little hush traveled before the gringo, and a little whisper formed in his wake.

Someone else had arrived from the direction of the border during the evening, and he had told a tale of a gringo outlaw who had escaped into Mexico that very day, and who was sought at an enormous price by his fellow gringos. The Americans would indeed offer a great fortune for his delivery. It needed no more than to rap a knife between his ribs and cart his cold body to the frontier. There the payment would be made, and what could be simpler?

But why was the great reward offered?

Because, said the bringer of news, the terrible rider of a gray horse had defied successfully the greatest wielders of guns north of the Rio Grande. At this the speculative light died in many eyes, and a certain fumbling at belts ceased. Because, with all their faults, the gringos were assuredly men of might with powder and lead. Peter Quince completed his walk in safety and returned to the tavern; and, though it was not very pleasant to Peter, it was good enough. He rolled onto the bed and was instantly asleep.

It was as black as pitch in the room when Peter suddenly awakened with a wildly hammering heart; but he was not surprised by this wakefulness in the middle of the night, for it had become his habit ever since the great price had been placed upon his head. Sometimes it seemed to him in his dreams that the world was heaping upon him a weight of raw gold which he had to carry upon his shoulders, and that this weight was the price of the reward which lay upon his head. He felt that he was being crushed to the earth by that burden and could stagger forward no longer beneath it. At this point in the nightmare he would awaken, just as he was awakening now, with perspiration rolling down his face and his nerves jumping. But tonight there was something to justify fear— as light footfalls sounded.

He had curled himself on the bed ready for a leap into the darkness, when he realized that the footfalls sounded from the floor above his room. He discovered this with a sigh of relief, amazed to find himself shaking from head to foot. Then he waited for the sound of the walking to die out above him, so that he might sleep again. But it did not stop. It continued softly, as of a man pacing backward and forward with the greatest care, fearful lest he should disturb anyone in the building, and yet every step caused creakings here and there.

For a round half hour, for an hour, Peter listened. He could have gone to sleep again had the noises been repeated at all regularly. But there was nothing regular about them. The footfalls went slowly, then quickly, then paused. They were for all the world like sounds one might make as one walked back and forth in the midst of an excited debate with a companion, now hurrying in the midst of anxious thought to bring up a new reason, now walking slowly, delivering an argument with the maximum force, and again coming to a full halt to listen to an expostulation. Yet there were no murmurs of voices to accompany those ghostly steps. They wandered on; back and forth and back and forth, and there was no sign of reason for the walking.

At last the strained nerves of Peter Quince could stand no more. He leaped from his bed, stepped into his boots, snatched gun and cartridge belt around him, jammed a hat upon his head and climbed the stairs to the floor above and to the room over his. There he listened again at the door, and the sounds were exactly such as those which he had heard from beneath. His anger grew as he listened. But when he tapped at the door there was no answer. He repeated the summons, this time kicking heavily with his foot, for his anger had passed all bounds at a single leap.

"Enter, señor!" called a faint voice from within.

Instantly he flung the door wide before him. What he saw was a room completely clothed in darkness except for the flickering light of a single candle, and this was placed on a stand near the door. As for the farther recesses of the room, they were almost completely lost in shadow, and it was only at the second glance that Peter made out a dim figure crowded into a far recess. His eye was more guided by the glint of a naked gun than by the shape of a discernible figure, but now he saw that a man stood there at bay, with a weapon in either hand, and his body was crouched in the manner of one who is driven to desperation by fear.

"What the devil," said Peter, forgetting his Spanish in the excitement of the moment, "is the meaning of all this ghost walking, friend?"

There was a gasp from the other.

"Are you English?" called a faint and shaken voice.

"American," said Peter.

"God be praised for that!"

"You talk as though there were something wrong," said Peter.

"Hush! Hush!" breathed the other. "Not so loud. If a word is heard, we are both no better than dead men!"

"A crazy man," said Peter to himself, as he stepped into the room and closed the door behind him. But he added aloud: "Now we're here together, and you can tell me what's wrong with you, partner. If you're an American, then we're bound to help one another in a strange land. Talk out as though you've known me five years instead of five seconds!"

"You are a thousand times kind!" whispered the other. "And yet, what if you should be—"

"Be what?"

"One of them!"

"One of whom?"

The man in the corner apparently made a great and reckless resolve. Suddenly he stepped forward and came into the center of the room. Peter could now see that he was young, good-looking in a lean-faced way, a man of some presence and a good deal of manifest gentility. But he was obviously in a blue funk. He mouthed his words in a way that showed his lips were thick with fear, and his eyes were feverishly bright and as narrow as the eyes of an animal.

"Put up your guns," suggested Peter, swallowing any scorn which he might have felt. For the sight of such fear made him grind his teeth lest any Mexican should dare to see an American with a white skin in such a nervous condition, to call it by no worse a name. "Put them up," he urged more heartily.

"I tell you," said the other, and he shrank back a little toward the wall, "I tell you that I am in the most mortal danger every instant. A bullet through the window—"

The color was washed out of his face by the thought.

"I tell you," said Peter gravely, "that you would be a rare shot indeed if you could hit anything while that—er—while that chill is making your hands shake so!"

The other looked down, as if he were realizing this truth for the first time.

"Right," he muttered. "You're double right about that. Couldn't send a bullet through that wall over there, and with their devilish knives—"

He flung the guns from him. They crashed one on top of the other on the bed, and he made a gesture of infinite repulsion. Then he walked straight up to Peter. The instant he put down the guns he seemed to have recovered much of his poise.

"Now, sir," he said, "if you have been hired to take a hand against me, I'm helpless and disarmed, as you see, and you can begin."

"Not at all helpless," insisted Peter. "You have your hands free." He added: "I give you my word that I'm simply coming here tonight because your walking kept me awake."

"Is that all?" gasped the other. "In the name of mercy, man, is that all? Sit down and welcome! Sit down and a thousand welcomes! Every minute you stay here with me is a gift of gold—a gift of priceless diamonds!"

10. MARTIN AVERY'S STORY

His extravagance and the shaking hands with which he now drew Peter toward a chair began to convince the latter that he had to do with a mere habitual coward. He saw that Peter was seated, and then he brought out cigars and a flask of brandy, crowding his welcome upon his guest.

"Tell me in five words," said Peter Quince, "whom do you fear?"

The lips of the other parted, but at the very thought of the words he was about to utter, his eyes widened and he shook his head. "I can't tell you that," he said.

"How the devil can I be of help to you," said Peter, "if you won't talk out?"

"Help?" said the other. "No, no! You cannot help me. No one can. Of course, I know that."

"What earthly good am I to you then?"

"What good is a puppy to a child who's afraid of the dark? He knows that the puppy can't help him, but still it comforts him."

There was something not at all flattering in this comparison. But Peter waited to learn more of his companion before he made any judgments.

"Tell me the story!" suggested Peter.

The other shook his head.

"I cannot do that."

"Very well," said Peter. "I leave you to your walk. I'm going back to bed."

There was a groan from his host and a frantic protest.

"But," said Peter reasonably enough, "I have come here with a wish to help you, and I don't intend to lose sleep unless I can do so. I've been here five minutes and have learned not even your name!"

"As for my name, you are welcome to it. It is Martin Avery."

"Mine is Peter Quince."

He watched the face of the other carefully, but it was plain that Martin Avery had been living in some place where the fame of Peter's long ride had not yet spread. They acknowledged one another, and Martin Avery continued: "If I were to tell you the story, do you know what would happen? A bullet would come through that window yonder and stop me."

"Here I am standing before the window," said Peter. "If a bullet jumps through this window it will have to hit me first."

He looked out as he spoke. The moon was shining now. It paved the patio with white; it laid silver upon the roof of the stable; it made the shadows under the patio arcade blacker than ink. There could not have been a more peaceful scene. He thought instinctively of Bad

Luck nosing at the last of his hay and preparing to lie down and sleep.

"You don't understand," said Martin Avery. "If the bullet didn't come through the window, it would come through the wall. They find a way of doing what they want to do."

"This is raving, Avery."

"If you stay in this country long you'll learn to agree with me! This is not the States, Quince."

"Very well."

"And yet why shouldn't I tell you at least part of what I've done? There's no harm in the beginning."

Peter took a chair and sat down. But, as he had promised, he faced the chair toward the window. And Avery drew back his own chair toward a corner. Fear had proceeded to such a point with him that he no longer even attempted to show the face and mere form of courage.

"Quince," said the narrator, "what I'm going to tell you will sound like a section out of a fairy story."

"I'll do my best to believe you."

"Very well. And, by Jove, it makes me feel better even to think of talking about it! In the first place, I graduated from college in engineering. And I tried to learn about irrigation."

"That sounds like a poor beginning for a fairy story," murmured Peter.

"You can't tell by the beginnings of things, not in the twentieth century!"

"That's true. Go ahead then, Avery."

"I did some work around the big dams in the Southwest. Built up a little name for myself, and then I spent a couple of years grinding at reclamation projects in California until I received the invitation to come down and handle the job for Señor Monterey. Of course you know about him?"

"Never heard the name."

"The devil! He's the richest man in Mexico."

"Is that so?"

"It is. His position and fortune have roots so old and so deep that even the revolutions don't get down to the bottom of them. They've shaken Señor Monterey, but they've never broken him. He's lost half, perhaps, but now he's on the way toward making it all back again and more on the side. That's where I come in."

"Go on," said Peter. "This sounds more like your promise in the beginning."

"I came down to look over the project. I reached the Monterey estate and found it like a little country set off by itself. The house is a palace, a regular castle. It was built up among the rocks in the days when it paid to have one's house useful as a fort. That must have been in the minds of the first Montereys, and Don Felipe found that so much money had been spent on the old building that he hadn't the heart to move out of it. There he lives still, perched up there on the top of a cliff, like an eagle on the stump of a tree. That's what he is, you know—a regular eagle.

"What the old boy wanted me to do was to look into the possibility of building a dam and reclaiming about five thousand acres from the desert. It would mean raising the value of that land from five dollars an acre or less to more than three hundred. Monterey would stand to clean up a cold million in our money, at the least. As a matter of fact, he was reasonably sure of getting an additional income of two hundred thousand dollars a year at a cost of a little more than twice that amount.

"The old fellow had seen the possibilities of the water supplies which were going to waste in his mountains. He had planned out the whole scheme. In truth, there wasn't much need of me at all. But modern education seems to have convinced everyone that common sense is not good enough to act on. A man has to have a professor's opinion on everything. So old Monterey get me down to give an opinion.

"It was as plain as the nose on a man's face. I needed ten minutes to see that the thing was feasible. But I thought it would be better to spend three days riding about, asking questions about the flow of water in the river, examining high-water marks, talking rainfall, and what not. At the end of the three days I gave my opinion and turned in a bill in which I had doubled all my estimates. Señor Monterey gave me a check for twice the amount I asked and then requested me to go ahead in drawing up a plan for the whole affair.

"I was established like a king, while the dam was being planned, and then while it was being built. Señor Monterey built me a house near the site of the dam—that is to say, on the other side of the range from his own establishment. He furnished that house from top to bottom. He gave me enough servants to have attended a king of England. I had three men to take care of half a dozen horses which were appropriated for my sole use. There was a swarm of servants in the kitchen, which I could never untangle. There were others at work on a garden, when Monterey discovered that I like flowers. By heavens, Peter Quince, they dug up plants out of the huge gardens of the old castle and carried them on the backs of burros, packed in loam and moss, to my house. They mined around young trees on the rainy side of the range, and they jolted them with great masses of dirt clinging around their roots, over the crest of the range in big carts and put them around the house which had been built for me.

"All of this was done because I had told Monterey, when I saw the site of the dam, that it would be a bleak spot to live in until the dam was actually built, and its water could be used. A garden and a young forest were planted around me. To give you an inkling of the courtesy of Monterey, when he discovered that I had a tooth for freshly killed game, he appointed two of his best men to do nothing but hunt through the mountains every day and bring me what they killed.

"I was like a king over my household. But, of course, they got out of hand. I could not abuse them fluently enough in Spanish, perhaps. So I told Monterey that, though I appreciated his kindness, I much preferred to have one servant and peace to twenty servants and a constant wrangle.

"He looked me in the eye and smiled. The next day there arrived at my house a little, bent, withered old man, with a head of silver hair and eyes which were almost lost in wrinkled lids. Then a solemn silence dropped upon my house. The servants actually walked in a different way. And when they looked at me they seemed to be afraid I might frown. The wheels of my household were so oiled that I began to forget that I was served by human hands. I never heard arguments in the kitchen or in the garden. I had nothing but the most scrupulous silence and courtesy around me.

"I tell you this to give you some understanding of Señor Monterey—that is to say, one side of him. There are other sides, but for a whole year I could not guess them. The dam was completed. I was still kept on to see what would happen to my dam and to my system of irrigation ditches when the water collected. It meant paying my salary for three months more, but three months is merely nothing to Monterey. He seems to be spending like a crazy man, and yet everything he touches turns to gold. Heaven alone knows how much he spent on my house, my grove of trees, my garden, my elaborate table. In return, I did for him the best work I have ever done in my life. That dam will stand forever, I think. And, instead of bringing five thousand acres under water, I brought eight thousand under by using two big pumps to raise the water to a higher level. However, I'll not bother you with details. Monterey spent lavishly on me to make me happy. He made me so happy that I became inspired for his sake.

"Then I went to him and told him that I must go home. He told me to go by all means. I told him it was good-bye. But he said that I must come again to see him after I had been among my own people. I went back to New York. What can you guess that the old rascal did? He sent one of his right-hand men to Manhattan. He rented an apartment for me. He secured a fine French chef. He hired the finest maids. He bought me, out of hand, a limousine and a ninety-horse-power runabout, with enough speed to race on a track.

"I have never known such generosity.

"These were merely little conveniences to make my stay in New York more comfortable. I wrote to Monterey and begged him to turn over his apartment to someone else—that I could not afford to appear in my old circle of New York friends in such a splendid setting which I could not afford to maintain. He wrote back that I was free to use, or not to use, the apartment, but that every day three meals would be prepared for me, the chauffeur would hold himself in readiness to answer my orders and my comfort would be served in every way. If I did not care to put my foot inside the door, I must not think that I in the least offended the señor. It was himself he was trying to please!

"That, I swear, is what he wrote to me. And what could I do? The temptation was too great. I entertained my friends in such style as I had never dreamed of. I was surrounded by the atmosphere of a prince; and how could I help but do my best to be the prince in very fact?"

He paused, with a sigh.

"You understand what was happening. Monterey still had uses for me, and he was attaching me inevitably to his service. I went about and looked here and there for work. I received a few good offers—very good offers, as a matter of fact—but I could not think of them seriously. I could not make up my mind to do without all of this luxury. And the end was that I went back to Monterey.

"He received me with open arms. I was entertained in his house royally. I tried to ask him what future use he could have for me, but he told me that he could not think of business for a fortnight after my return. We must do nothing but celebrate the occasion."

Martin paused for an instant.

"A hypocrite of the first water, eh?" murmured Peter Quince.

"I hardly know," said Martin Avery. "I can't condemn him offhand. I believe that he enjoys acting so much that he himself hardly knows when he's actually serious. At any rate, the two weeks of entertainment came to an end, and on the very last day of it I went to see him in his private suite of rooms. They were like the personal suite of an emperor. They were like jewel boxes rather than rooms. But what I saw there makes no difference, with the exception of one thing—for there on the wall I saw hanging her picture!"

"Well," said Peter, "for a time I thought this was really going to be a story without a heroine."

"Without her," said Martin Avery, "I had as soon die here and now!"

"And yet aren't you running away from her?"

"I'll come back again! There's nothing under the sun that can keep me from going back to her again."

"But the picture!" urged Peter Quince.

"I'll tell you about it in a moment," nodded the other and began to smoke rapidly at a cigarette, sending up a thick blue-brown mist behind which his frowning face of thought was barely distinguishable.

11.   A LONG-BLADED KNIFE

"As for her face," said Martin Avery, "that, of course, doesn't count. I couldn't describe it in the first place, and, if I succeeded, you wouldn't begin to believe me."

"Perhaps not," said Peter. "You're probably seeing love and not a woman."

"That sounds very wise for a chap of your age," said Martin Avery, with something of a sneer, "but if you should ever see her—"

"No fear of that. I never shall."

"But if you should, the same thing would happen to you. What I say now, and swear to you soberly, is that her face is perfect; her smile is perfect; her hands, her throat are perfect. There is a cloud of beauty blowing about her like the fragrance around a bog of perfume."

"Now you become poetic, and you can't expect me to believe."

"I can't talk about her in everyday words, but when you see her, Quince, you'll know that I've simply understated everything. Old Monterey saw me transfixed before the picture.

" 'Who,' said I to him, 'is this?'

" 'I'll let you guess,' said he.

" 'It is some woman whom you knew when you were young,' said I, growing sick inside my heart.

" 'Does she look old-fashioned?' said he.

" 'She looks as if she had lived forever!' said I.

"At this Monterey jumped up from his chair. 'Have I ever spoken to you about her?' he snapped at me.

" 'Never,' said I.

" 'Then where did you learn those words?'

" 'Out of her picture.'

" 'Well,' said Monterey, 'let it rest there! Let it rest there!'

"But it was plain that he was very much excited, as he walked up and down the room. He stopped at length and began to talk of something else. He would take me tomorrow to show me the new work which he wanted me to plan. As he talked, he became enthusiastic again. There were other desert tracts in Mexico which were merely waiting for the water to touch the soil. I was the man to give them the touch of enchantment.

"However, I knew that I had touched a tender spot in the mind of Monterey when I had talked about the girl of the picture. But I was too excited myself to care very much for the excitement of Monterey. I dreamed of the girl that night. The next day Monterey and I went over the mountains on a long trip of exploration. We were gone twenty days. In that time, we covered four hundred miles of trail, and Monterey had taken me to half a dozen places where there were possibilities for reclamation projects, each as large as the one I had already completed for him. I saw before me a life's work. I saw fame and fortune calling me. And, as I began to paint the picture of what these deserts could mean to Monterey, the old man seemed drunk with excitement. He took my hand with such a grip that I thought all the bones had crumbled away under his touch."

"You said he was an old man?" asked Peter.

"He's fifty—sixty—I don't know which. His hair is white. That makes him seem older. But he still has the strength of an athlete."

"Very odd," said Peter.

"On the way back to his estate we planned the conquest of the agricultural wealth of Mexico's deserts. We saw a perfect heaven of undeveloped possibilities. So we came one evening to a crest from which the big house on the top of the cliff was visible. Monterey gave one glance to it and then cried out: 'She is there!' and spurred his horse down the slope like a madman.

"I waited to examine the house with my glass. All that I could see was strange about the place was a bright blue flag with a red cross on it, which fluttered from one of the square-topped towers."

"Towers?" said Peter Quince.

"Didn't I tell you that the place was a regular castle? Then I followed Monterey, but I could not catch up with him. At the entrance to the house—or, rather, at the bottom of the trail which leads directly up to the house—I saw his horse standing, covered with foam, swaying from side to side with exhaustion. I gave my own horse to a servant.

" 'What has happened?' I asked.

" 'I cannot understand, señor,' says he.

"I repeated my question in good Spanish, but the rascal had the assurance to smile in my face and tell me that he could not understand. So I knew that he had his orders, and that I should gain nothing from him or from any other person in the house. In some way Monterey had laid them all under a fear of him, which was like the fear of death. I really believe that if they had their choice the servants would attack the black angel of death rather than their master.

"I went up to my room in the house. At dinner I waited anxiously for the appearance of Monterey and Mary."

"Mary?" cried Peter suddenly. "Did you say that her name was Mary?"

"I did. What of that?"

"Nothing—except that I have an idea that I shall see her before very long."

"You had better throw yourself over the next cliff than attempt to see her, my friend! Let me tell you what happened to me. Mary did not come to dinner that night. Monterey himself appeared and made excuses. She was tired from her long journey. She would appear in the morning. In the meantime, Monterey was thick with apologies for having left me so abruptly on the trail. In fact, his color heightened a little, as he spoke, and it was no wonder. For I could not avoid the conclusion that old Monterey was actually planning to marry this young girl!

"In the meantime, he began to talk business at a furious rate. All evening he kept it up and seemed to become so enthusiastic that he decided I should leave the house the next morning and go on to the first of the irrigation projects to lay my plans for the dam and the ditches.

"I went to bed convinced that I could never live as a happy man unless I had seen the face of this Mary. I could not sleep. It was partly Mary and partly, I confess, it was the dread of El Tigre."

"Of whom?" asked Peter.

"You have heard of El Tigre surely!"

"The Mexican bandit, you mean?"

"That's the one!"

"What has he to do with Monterey?"

"A great deal, but in what way I haven't been able to make out. That's one of the mysteries that hang around Monterey and his house. I wish to heaven that it were the only one. But so far as I could make out, El Tigre is the fly in the ointment of Monterey. When even the servants mention that name around the house of Monterey they turn and look behind them. I give you my word that I have seen them do it in the middle of the day! El Tigre had been recently seen in the neighborhood, and the thought of him made me nervous.

"I got up after a while, dressed and went out for a walk. The place I chose was a queer one. I went out an old door and began to pace up and down on the narrow ledge between the base of the wall of the building and the lip of the precipice. I passed around the part of the house which is now in use—you have to understand that the whole structure is spread out over a great deal of ground —and so I came around behind the wall of the oldest part of the house.

"It was not a place or a time that was particularly healthy for bad nerves. As a matter of fact, I was in a blue funk. You'll think me a great coward, Quince, but, when the pinch comes, I think you'll find that I do at least as well as the average."

"I'm sure of that," lied Peter smoothly.

"I went along with half my mind on the beauty of Mary and the rest of it wrapped up in the thought of El Tigre. He is such a daring and relentless devil, you know, that nothing is too bold for him. He has been known to steal right down to the house of Monterey and carry away men."

"Carry them away!" echoed Peter, amazed, and with good reason.

"Of course. He needs recruits for his band now and then, and when he hears of a likely man, he simply goes and takes him. Isn't that clear?"

"He must have nerves of chilled steel!"

"He has no fear at all. I understand that some lucky men are equipped in that way. I'm not one of the lot! But to get back to the house of Monterey. I say that I had passed around a corner of the old section of the house so that I had a glimpse of the base of the cliff, and there I saw a man strolling easily along. I paid no attention to that for the moment. I went on around the next corner of the house and looked down again. But this time I stopped. For the man who had been walking along at the foot of the rock was no longer there!"

Even as he remembered that fact, Martin Avery bit his lip and fluttered a shaken hand across his forehead.

"He'd stepped back among the rocks?" suggested Peter.

"The face of that rock was almost as smooth as the wall of a brick house. There was nothing behind which he could have stepped. I stared across the valley. But he was not there. He could not have flattened himself against the sand, because the moon was very bright, and at the same time it threw a slanting light, so that every little rock which projected at all above the surface of the white-sanded floor of the valley cast a clear black shadow. I could spot every one, as though they were marked with ink on white paper. A man could not have hidden himself away from me. It was impossible!"

"A miracle then had snatched him away," sneered Peter.

"I went down to investigate," said Martin Avery. He rubbed his hands to get back the warm blood. "When I think of it I wonder now how I ever was able to find the courage to do it, but I tell you now that I went down to the foot of the cliff, following down the first of the long and winding flights of steps which are cut into the rock. Even to go down that flight of steps would have been too

much for me in the daylight, but in the night, in spite of
the recent mysteries of the coming of the girl, the strange
conduct of Monterey about her and the presence of the
outlaw, El Tigre, according to the report, I was able to
go down those stairs without so much as the tremor of a
hand. At the foot of the cliff I looked around to see what
was what. It was not hard to trace my man. His footsteps
were sharply defined in the sand by means of the shadows
which the moonlight pooled in the little hollows. I followed those black shadows up to the foot of the cliff, and
there I saw that they came to a halt, as though my man
had walked deliberately into the heart of the rock!"

"The devil!" whispered Peter Quince.

"And I knew all at once that that was exactly what he
had done. I began to fumble around on the rough face
of the rock, tugging here, jerking there, working at every
crevice with my fingertips until the blood came—and then
something gave way, and, without a sound, a section of
the heavy rock wheeled aside. I remember that I was
amazed at the smoothly chiseled edges of the rock, as
they were exposed. That tunnel seemed to be hewed into
the living stone, and I saw at the end of the passage—"

A whisper entered the room through the window. There
was a soft thud, and in the stout adobe of the wall, just
above the head of Martin Avery, appeared a long and
slender-bladed knife which was now quivering so violently that it filled the air in the room with the noise of
its soft murmuring.

12.   A WINDOW-SILL WARNING

MARTIN AVERY was as good as his promise to be better
than Peter expected in a crisis. The instant he saw the
knife humming in the wall above his head he leaped for
the table in the corner, scooped a gun off it, and rushed to
the window; but fast as his motions had been, Peter
Quince was far more swift, and he arrived at the window
and stared down into the patio.

There was nothing in sight. No one stirred in the patio. A dog was curled in the direct center of it, sleeping in the moonshine, with a black shadow sleeping beside it on the ground. Otherwise there was no living thing in view. He glanced up to the broad eaves. That was the only possible explanation. Someone could have lowered himself from the roof to the window, heard the conversation, and hurled the deadly knife.

"We'll raise the house!" cried Peter, starting for the door.

"Don't do that!" he begged.

"Why the devil not?"

"What happens to a wolf when it's wounded in the midst of a hungry pack?"

"Eaten, say the story books. I never saw it happen."

"That's what would happen to me down here if they found out that Monterey was my enemy! They'd feel that an open season was declared on me, and every man within a hundred miles would know that if he got me the rich man would reward him and protect him."

"How could they know that Monterey had a hand in it? And how can even you be sure, Avery?"

"Is it probable that men would be wandering around the countryside, throwing knives at me?"

He smiled; and ever since the throwing of the knife he had been actually calm in manner, though he was very pale.

"That's true enough," said Peter. "Still, how could the others know that?"

"There'll be some sign if he's really from Monterey."

He walked to the other side of the room and wrenched the knife from the adobe.

"Ah!" he said. "There you are, just as I had expected!" He extended the knife to Peter, and the latter saw a silver "M" stamped into the haft of the dagger.

" 'M' for murder," said Peter gloomily. "What the devil sort of a country is this?"

"A good-enough country when you once know its ways."

Peter growled his indignation. "What sort of law is there?" he exclaimed indignantly, and then he bit his lip, remembering that he had fled from his own country. "Put up the knife, and no one will know that this terrible Monterey has been after you," suggested Peter.

"There may be some other trace. Ah, here you are!" exclaimed Avery, as he pointed to the sill of the window, to which he had wandered. When Peter joined him he saw that a shallow "M" had been slashed on the sill of the window, perhaps by the keen edge of the same knife which a moment later had been flung at the head of the victim.

"A mighty queer business!" said Peter. "Here is a man who sends out a fellow to commit a murder, and the man leaves behind him the clues which will point straight at Monterey as the guilty man."

"Why?" asked Avery, who, now that the blow had fallen, seemed fully as cool under the strain as was Peter himself. "Anyone can commit a murder and then carve the initials of whomever he pleases on the scene of the crime. Do you think it will mean anything to a jury? Besides, what jury will convict Monterey, or even one of his employees?"

"You're helpless against him then?"

"I'm a dead man, Quince. He'll get me before morning!"

"Nonsense!"

"When that 'M' is seen, everyone will know that he's after us."

"Then scrape the initial off the window sill."

"It's too late for that, I'm afraid."

With this he stepped to the door, jerked it open, and then uttered a faint exclamation, pointing dramatically down to the floor of the hall just in front of him. Peter hurried to his side and saw, cut carefully and underlined with an elaborate flourish, a great capital "M" sunk in the floor.

"That's his brand put on me," sighed Avery.

"How could the rascal have had the nerve to crouch there for ten minutes at his work? It must have taken that long for him to carve it."

"Ah," said Avery, "the men who serve Monterey forget such a thing as fear."

"He employs bunglers, however," said Peter Quince.

Suddenly the face of Avery lighted. "But was it really bungling?" he asked. "Wasn't that miss intentional?"

"What can you mean by that?"

"Do you recall at what point in my story I was stopped by the shining of that knife in the air?"

"Of course I remember. You were about to describe what lay in the passage in the rock."

"And there the knife was thrown!"

"It was."

"Then that is what is taboo!" He leaped from his chair, with a groan of relief. "I am simply warned that I must not chatter about the things I know."

"Are you actually going to pay any attention to that sort of thing, Avery?"

"Of course I am going to pay attention!"

"I'm robbed of the rest of the story then," smiled Peter.

"You are, Quince. I only hope that telling you what I have told does not mean that you are put in danger."

"Of what?"

"Of Monterey."

"Hang Monterey and the crowd that follows him!"

"Hush! That's blasphemy in this part of the country!"

"I'll get along in spite of Señor Monterey, Avery."

But Avery had already half forgotten him. "It was certainly a warning," he said, with growing happiness; "and if he sent me a warning it means that I have nothing to fear so long as I do not talk."

"Why the brands on the window sill and floor?"

"To tell people to beware of me—that I am not friendly to Monterey; but the way it is underlined, I imagine, shows that I am not to be attacked seriously except by his own men. Yes, that must be it!"

He went back to the window in feverish haste. "There's the same waved line under this 'M'," he said. "That must be the sign of amity."

"Without the underlining it means plain murder?" asked Peter.

"Exactly that!"

"Then you talk no more?"

"Not a syllable!"

"Come, come, Avery!"

"You may call it cowardice, but there's where I stick!"

"Very well then—good night."

"Good night, Quince. Thank you for coming up!"

"You'll sleep securely now?"

"As securely as though I had never known what the word danger meant."

"Happy dreams," said Peter, and straightway left the room.

Peter did not know whether to despise the childishness of Avery, or to respect the strange courage with which it was intermingled. Or perhaps, he decided, this was the result of knowing the country and the people who lived in it. Slowly Peter went down the stairs and returned to his own room. When he opened the door, the light flooded out across something white. He looked down on it again, amazed, stunned by what he saw. But there could be no doubt about it. It was an "M" cut into the wood, with all the care of that initial in the floor of the hallway above him. But in this case there was no underlining. In this case there was to be no mere warning then, but he was to receive the dagger in his throat!

13. "EL TIGRE"

AT FIRST he laughed and, striding into his room, banged the door heavily behind him. But suddenly he found himself shivering with apprehension in the darkness, and the four corners of the room seemed to be filled with unseen shapes. He gritted his teeth and made himself light a candle. He stood scowling at his hand, lest that member of his body should dare to tremble against his will; and when he saw that it did not he permitted his eyes to glance up and rove around the room in search of danger.

There was none. Nothing stirred in the chamber, and now he went to the window to look down into the patio and, leaning out to breathe the fresh air and to watch the silver of the flooding moonshine, he rested his left hand on something with rough, sharp edges on the wood of the sill. He removed the hand and looked down, and there was another "M" staring up to his face.

"A lot of childish trickery," said Peter. "And I'll balance this against 'em any time." So saying, all unconsciously he slipped his Colt into his hand, but the instant the weapon was balanced, he realized that there was something wrong with it. It was light, strangely light in the magazine; and Peter had lived so constantly with a gun in his hand that the difference of a hair meant a great deal to him. He turned out the bullets anxiously, and the alteration was at once apparent. His gun was filled with blanks, and the honest slugs had been taken away. He was as helpless with the revolver in his hand as he would have been with a painted wooden toy.

It would be pleasant to say that our hero shrugged his shoulders, refilled the chambers of his revolver, threw himself on the bed and was instantly asleep; but, as a matter of fact, Peter sat for a long time turning the problem back and forth in his mind. And the longer he thought the more the pricking passed up and down his spine. Of course, the only time that the cartridges could have been switched was during the period when he was asleep in his room. Someone must have entered and remained long enough to take the cartridge belt and the gun from the chair where they rested beside his bed. Someone must have done this so cautiously that he heard not a sound, and yet he knew that he slept with hardly more than one eye shut. It was to him incredible that he should have been so surprised.

But why should they have tampered with his gun in the first place? At least, why should the emissaries of Monterey have taken any trouble with him, unless they knew that he was an American, and they had worked on the long chance that he might be tempted to come to the rescue of his fellow countryman? And when he had gone up to the room of Avery, why had they determined to pin upon him this signal to the attack—this unadorned initial which, according to Avery, must mean that he was exposed to instant assault?

This question made him probe carefully, but he could come to no satisfactory answer, except that they had indeed overheard the conversation which took place between

him and Avery. They had overheard, though the walls
were so thick, and they had decided, these unseen minis-
ters of Señor Monterey, that the gringo must be disposed
of.

While he turned these thoughts in his mind, he was
reloading his revolver. They had marked him down,
knowing only that he would be more formidable than
Martin Avery, should the chance come for him to get into
action. They contented themselves with warning Avery
away, but they would strike Peter Quince down on the instant.

He went back to his window and gloomily contem-
plated the sleeping dog and the black pool of shadow
beside the creature. The peaceful scene beneath the moonshine made his own danger seem greater than ever. And
yet he could not flee. In the first place, there was a
compatriot above him who might be in the greatest need
of assistance. In the second place, Bad Luck was sadly in
need of food and rest.

What Peter finally did was to lock his door, draw away
his bed quietly from the corner in which it had been standing and lie down facing the window. He determined to
spend the rest of the night in this fashion, fully dressed,
his eyes upon the window and his gun in his hand. The
result was that he was almost instantly soundly asleep,
asleep without dreaming. Instead of a dream he wakened
again—it was late in the night, or very close to the morning—to the sound of a horse stamping in the patio outside.
For it was really a courtyard rather than a patio, and
those who came to the tavern rode straight into it.

Yet who could be arriving at this time of night? Peter
was about to compose himself for sleep again when, as
he closed his eyes, he remembered that in his former
sleep he had heard something other than the stamping of
a horse. It had been a choked and short sound, like the
beginning of a cry, incompleted because a hand was
clapped across the mouth. There was fear and deadly pain
in that sound, and it was this which must have wakened
him from his sleep, with a heart beating so strongly.

Now he rose and passed to the window. The quiet had
departed from the dust of the patio. Four horses stood
there. The saddles of two were already occupied. Into a

third saddle a giant of a man was lifting a man whose hands were tied behind his back. He threw the fellow up with a wonderful ease and secured his feet beneath the belly of the horse, with a quickly passed rope from stirrup to stirrup. In the meantime, Peter watched him with a fascinated interest. He had never seen the like of this big man before. It seemed to him, indeed, that two men rolled together could not have made a unit as formidable as he.

His face was turned to the window most of the time, and it was the face of a hawk, deep-featured, with out-thrusting nose and chin, and sunken eyes. The latter still glittered out from the shadow of his brows and from the double shadow of the wide hat upon his head. He must have stood fully six feet and four inches, and he had a huge head and a sweeping pair of shoulders and long, thick arms to match. But the rest of his body tapered off; just as one sometimes sees an athlete, heavy as a prize fighter above and light as a distance runner below. There were crushing weight and power about the arms and shoulders of the stranger, and yet his total bulk would not be too great for a horse to carry far and swiftly. Certainly it would not be too much for such a horse as the chestnut monster who stood nearby—a full seventeen hands in height and muscled for both speed and power.

Having secured his victim, the big man tossed to one of the other two horsemen the reins, and the pair closed up on either side of the bound man, while the leader vaulted into the saddle on the big chestnut. They were about to start when the prisoner worked the gag from his teeth and screamed: "Help! Quince—in heaven's name, help!"

And there was poor Martin Avery, who had been so certain that no more harm was before him—there he was being led away, no doubt, so that he could be murdered at the leisure of these villains! Peter did not pause to think. He was through the window in a flash, hung for an instant from the sill by his fingertips and then dropped into the dust beneath.

One of the dark-faced fellows who sat beside Avery had drawn a revolver and was pumping bullets wildly in the direction of Peter. He heard them thudding into the wide adobe wall of the tavern. And, like echoes of their landing, voices wakened here and there, and wild cries began to ring through the house. But the bullets were flying wild. Peter was more interested, as a matter of fact, in what the second man was doing to Martin Avery, for he was striking savagely at the head of Martin with the butt of a gun, and suddenly the young engineer slumped forward in the saddle. Whether he were dead or merely stunned, Peter could not tell.

These things Peter saw, as he dropped to the earth and crouched there an instant behind the veil of the dust which his fall had caused to billow up. But he saw that his first bullet must be for neither of the two subordinates. It must be saved for the leader. The big man had not stirred in his saddle after the cry of Martin Avery. But, with his reins in his left hand, and his right hand dropped upon his hip lightly, he awaited the developments of the fight. And there was something so lordly, so consciously invincible about his bearing, that Peter felt his heart shrink in spite of himself. Yes, he who had so dearly loved battle for all these years now found himself drawing back in a crisis!

He fought himself forward with a snarl, leaped clear of the dust mist and snatched at his gun. And he saw the big man reach for a weapon at the same instant. He could understand now why the other had waited. It was his own private code of honor which forbade him seizing at a gun before his enemy had reached in the same fashion. It was the pride of the marauder that his speed and his surety were greater than that of any other man.

About all these things Peter thought while he made his draw. He had time for all of this, though the draw was a mere jerk of the wrist and a flicker of swift fingers that snapped the heavy revolver out and set it barking from his hip. Perhaps amazement had made him a trifle slower; or perhaps the fall from the window ledge above him made him a bit bewildered. He felt capable of doing as well as he had ever done in his life, with the memory of Avery's cry still ringing at his ear; but when his gun was out, the gun of the big man was out before his. The gun of the stranger roared, there was a clang of metal at Peter's very ear and blackness dropped over his brain.

What happened was the sheerest luck. The slug of lead had been bound for the breast of Peter with all good intent, but on the way it struck the revolver in his hand, jerked it out of his fingers and threw the heavy gun up against the side of his head with stunning force. He dropped upon his back. When he sat up again, the pounding of hoofs was melting into the thinnest distance. Others had run into the patio. He saw people pointing, as they ran toward him, and the name on their lips was: "El Tigre! El Tigre!"

It was that famous outlaw then whom he had encountered. Then gentle hands were laid upon him, and he was told to lie down. He was promised that a priest would be sent for.

"But—why," asked Peter, "should I have a priest?"

"To take you gently out of this life and make you sure of the life hereafter, señor!" said the kind voice of the woman who owned the tavern.

"But," said Peter, "I have not the slightest intention of dying."

With this he shook himself clear from their hands and stood up. There was a volley of exclamations.

"You are not dying—you are not hurt? Where did the bullet enter your body?"

Peter ground his teeth. He was not used to pity. Now he picked up his revolver, dropped it into the holster, then picked up his hat and slapped it upon his head.

"I stumbled and fell," declared Peter smoothly enough, "and when I fell I struck my head against the wall of the tavern. That's why I lay there, and that's the only reason I didn't blow the head off that rascal, El Tigre— which is what I shall do the moment I can get in touch with him."

They seemed stricken dumb by these assertions. And from a broken phrase here and there he gathered that El Tigre never failed to kill when he fired—that there was a sort of superstition in the countryside that he could not fail, because he fired with charmed bullets. So an awe-stricken ring formed around Peter Quince, and he was barely able to break through and get up to his room. At the threshold he paused in bewilderment, hardly thinking that he could have reached the right door. For the deeply graven "M" which had been sunk into the wood of the hall floor had disappeared! He went into his bedroom feeling that magic was floating in the air of Mexico.

14. JUAN GARIEN

WHEN HE ROSE in the morning the first thing he did was to examine with care the floor in front of his door, and he soon came to an understanding of the miracle. For he found that the wood had been planed down around the spot where the letter had been incised, and over the planing dirt had been ground in so that the spot would not show to the casual eye. He examined his window sill also, and he discovered that the letter had been removed from this wood, too. What could it mean unless that the danger which had been threatening him from Monterey was gone? Or, perhaps, the letter had been removed at the moment he was confronting El Tigre, when it was thought that his end had come.

The whole affair was very strange. Peter decided that the best way to confront it was to forget all about it. And, having done this with a shrug of his shoulders, he went down to the stable to look after the wants of Bad Luck. He found the gray stallion wonderfully changed. It was the first time in whole weeks that Bad Luck had enjoyed so long a rest, such grain, such hay, so much clear, pure water! And already it seemed the gaunt line of his belly had filled out; his ribs were less prominent; his eye had gained in fire; and his neck was proudly arched.

Bad Luck followed Peter out into the little corral which adjoined, and they played a game together—a game terrible to behold, in which the part of Peter was to race around the corral wildly, as though in fear of death from the plunging hoofs and the snapping teeth of the stallion just behind him. But, swerving from side to side, he managed to avoid destruction, and in the end, with a leap high into the air, he landed upon the back of Bad Luck, as the stallion trumpeted his happiness with a neigh that rang across the village.

It was a childish game, but after all, Peter was only twenty-two. When he looked around him, panting and laughing, he found that he was being watched by a large audience. It was composed of boys and girls and young men from the village. Bare-footed, or wriggling their toes in sandals, they had drawn close into a semicircle, their eyes glittering with wonder.

"He could be a matador!" said a girl's voice, as the dust of the frolic blew slowly away from the corral.

"But look," said another. "The horse was only playing like a dog."

"Is there such a thing as an evil eye?"

"Hush!" said someone of the older children. "He'll hear you and then—"

They were reduced to utter silence and fear. And now a peon advanced in front of the others. He was a fellow of fine stature and fine bearing, but his clothes were rags. He had on a white cotton tunic and trousers, but the latter were frayed to shreds as high as his brown knees. He was furnished with a straw sombrero, on the one side of whose band was thrust a bunch of corn husks for cigarettes, and on the other side was a quantity of tobacco leaf for the same purpose. In fact, as he now came to the fence of the corral, he was extracting a film of corn husk from the one side and between his palms pulverizing a sufficient quantity of the tobacco. He lighted a cigarette; but at the same time, seeing that Peter was paying some attention to him, he let the cigarette go out in the violence of his greetings and in the profusion of his good words and of his smiles.

"Ah, sir," said the peon, "it is plain to be seen who is the happiest man in the whole world, and that is he who has a charm to turn bullets and another to enchant horses."

"Well," said Peter, "you are sure that I can turn bullets?"

"Did not El Tigre miss?" said the other.

"To be sure," said Peter. "He missed because I stumbled!"

"Ah, yes—ah, yes!" cried the peon. "Señor will say that. He will explain it away. But we all know! If he had only fallen, would not El Tigre have stayed and killed him as he lay there? But, no! We can see and understand! El Tigre was frightened when the strong charm turned his bullet!"

"Have it your own way," said Peter, and he rolled a cigarette and drummed his heel lightly against the side of Bad Luck.

"And the horse, too!" cried the peon.

Peter shrugged his shoulders. If he was to be made out supernatural, there was no good reason why he should not enjoy the game as it was being played.

"Will you call him down for me?" said the peon, and he pointed far above his head.

Peter Quince looked up, and far above him in the pale, thin blue of the upper sky hung a pendant speck of black which was a hunting hawk.

"Do you think I could call him down?" asked Peter.

"Of course, señor."

"But I promise you that I cannot!"

The other shrugged his shoulders and smiled wisely into the face of Peter.

"I am sorry señor has not that power," he said. "And yet," he added, "it is a pity for the other Americano."

"I shall bring him back safe and sound," lied Peter Quince, feeling that he must rise to the level at which the peon expected him to stand.

Here the other turned his back suddenly and called to the children, who had been crowding closer: "Get home, every one of you! The señor is weary of your faces. If you stay, he will call down the hawk to pick out your eyes."

They scattered with shrill little cries of fear.

"You will buy me a bad name with them," protested Peter.

"It is safer to be feared by children than to be loved by them," said the peon.

Peter studied his face with a greater interest. He was a handsome rascal, with eyes as bright as beads of jet and a fountain of energy in each of them.

"You are a wise fellow," said Peter Quince.

He was thanked with a bow.

"And where have you learned such politeness?"

"I have used my eyes."

"What is your name, my friend?"

"Juan Garien."

"Will you tell me, Juan, why the devil you have come out to pay so much attention to me this morning?"

"Ah," said Juan Garien, "it is because I wish to see closely the man who has done such a great thing."

"Is it so great to meet El Tigre and live to talk about it?"

"Of course, the señor knows. He is the first."

"Juan, that isn't what brought you here."

"What else could it be? Why else should I have come to see you, señor?"

"Answer that yourself, Juan."

"Very well, I must tell the truth. But you have borrowed the eye of that hawk. You are looking through me and into my heart. But the truth is, señor, that I was hungry and needed a breakfast."

"You shall have one, Juan."

He tossed Juan Garien a shiny silver dollar which the latter caught deftly out of the air and then rubbed between both his palms, as though to make sure that it was real. Then he took off his hat and pressed it against his breast.

"Señor," he said, "Our Lady guard you!"

"I've no doubt," said Peter Quince, "that you are still lying to me, Juan. Nevertheless, I had rather be amused than correct."

Here Juan Garien grinned broadly. "If you are a dollar happier," he said, "I am a dollar richer. Adios."

"Adios. Eat well, Juan."

"And how long does El Tigre live?"

Peter started.

"What makes you think he will die soon?"

"Tush, señor, cannot anyone tell that with ease? El Tigre dared to shoot at you, and then he has fled. But fleeing cannot save him! He must be hunted down, and then—"

"Juan, I have not the slightest idea of hunting down El Tigre."

Juan waved both his graceful hands.

"That is, of course, the truth, and yet one will sometimes doubt even the truth. Is that not so?"

"Perhaps."

Juan Garien drew out a clasp-knife and with it began to slice absently at the side of the post on which he was leaning.

"And there are others, señor, who are sure that you will hunt El Tigre."

"Is that so? They are wrong, Juan."

"I shall wager all that I have that El Tigre does not live until winter."

"You are a foolish fellow, Juan."

"Perhaps."

"But have you a friend who could take a message to this El Tigre?"

"Of course not, señor."

"But truly—and for five pesos, Juan Garien?"

"For five pesos—that is money which can buy a great deal even from a man who is afraid."

"I hope so, Juan. You will find me a friend, then?"

"I shall myself be that friend, señor!"

"Then, Juan, go find this El Tigre and tell him from me that he is a dog, and not a tiger."

"Ah!" murmured Juan.

"Tell him that I am coming to hunt him."

"I shall, señor, even if he puts his claws in me the next moment."

"Tell him that I shall stretch his hide on the rocks and feed his body to the coyotes and buzzards. And you may add anything else that you can think of, Juan."

"I have one or two small thoughts."

"I'll wager that you have. But here is the money."

"A thousand prayers for señor."

"But how shall I know that you'll do what I've asked you to do?"

"I have left the proof on the post that the señor may see!"

So saying, he fled away at an easy and long-striding run which showed that there was a wealth of Indian blood in the veins of Juan Garien. Peter hurried to the post and there found that the knife of Juan had carved out the rough outlines of a letter "M."

It was as if he could trust Juan.

15. AN EXCHANGE OF MESSAGES

PERHAPS JUAN GARIEN may have been hungry for his breakfast, but he was far hungrier to deliver his message. He sped across the low and rounded hills near the village and never slackened his rapid trot until he had covered seven miles of country. By that time he had dropped into a narrow valley, through the center of which trickled a muddy rivulet, and on the bank of the rivulet was a shack which looked like a dog house rather than a human habitation. Yet to this Juan Garien traveled, and, pausing fifty yards away, he called. Instantly the proprietor of the house came forth. He was a very old man, withered and time-dried, but still erect and bright of eye. He raised a hand in greeting to Juan Garien.

"Pedro Rincon," said the younger man, "I am happy to find you here."

"You have come a long distance in haste," said Pedro Rincon. "Why have you run to me, Juan Garien?"

"I have news for your master."

"I have no master, Juan."

"None?"

"Saving our Father in heaven."

"Pedro, I can name another."

"Do so then."

"El Tigre."

The face of the old man did not alter.

"We have known for a long time," said Juan, "that you serve him."

"You and the others who work for the Monterey?"

"That is it."

"I am still safe," said Pedro calmly. "So long as El Tigre is living, so long you will fear his hand and the length of his arm, and a hundred of you living together will not be able to harm him or any of his men."

"And this may be true," said the other.

"Ay, and it *is* true. Those are brave men who serve Monterey."

"Do you think I am a coward, Pedro Rincon?"

"You will become one. For when the heart of a man is bought with silver and gold, his courage is sold with it."

"How were you bought by El Tigre?"

"By kindness and by faith and by honor."

"What has he done for you?"

"When my boy was caught in the revolution, and they would have hanged him for a traitor, it was the money of El Tigre that bought him the death of an honest man by bullets and a firing squad!"

"And for this you are very thankful to El Tigre?"

"For this my life is his life!"

"Then, Pedro Rincon, I shall tell you a thing that will make your blood thick."

"It cannot be of El Tigre."

"I shall tell you that he has missed his spring!"

Pedro recoiled a little toward the door of the hut, and then he raised his hand for silence, but immediately another man stooped through the low door and straightened to the full of a great height before Juan Garien. And Juan's face turned to a pale yellow with fear. His cheeks sucked in, like the cheeks of a cadaver, and his skin became puckered.

"Do you know me?" asked the tall man.

Juan Garien fell upon his knees.

"Mercy!" he breathed.

"You are a fool," said the big man. "Stand up! I have never struck a coward."

Juan Garien rose uncertainly to his feet.

"What have you to say to me?"

"Nothing."

"Speak, Juan Garien!"

"It is word from a gringo."

"Tell me that."

"It is from Señor Peter Quince."

"From whom?" cried El Tigre.

He strode across to the shaking Juan and seized him by the shoulder. "From whom?" he repeated. There was only a limp weight depending from his hand.

"Señor Peter Quince. It is the name he is given."

El Tigre loosed his grip, and Juan dropped loosely to the earth, cringing there.

"It is a lie!" cried El Tigre.

"Yes, yes!" breathed Juan. "It is whatever El Tigre wishes his name to be!"

El Tigre drew out a wallet and opened the mouth of it. He poured a little chiming heap of golden coins into the great hard palm of his hand.

"Look!" he said.

"I see, I see!" moaned Juan Garien.

"Now tell me the truth!"

"I swear to the Holy Virgin. He has called himself Peter Quince. But if El Tigre wishes, then I say that he lied, and his name is some other thing; I do not know what!"

"From what direction did he ride in?"

"From the north."

"Ah! Is there any word of him?"

"Only one man came in and made a big talk."

"Of what?"

"That Peter Quince was a great man-killer from among the Americanos. Two hundred thousand pesos is the price they will pay for him, living or dead! Consider that, señor!"

"A lie," groaned El Tigre.

"Ah, yes, a lie—a lie!" stammered Juan Garien.

"Stand up again, fool!" He dragged him to his feet. "You are going back to Peter Quince?"

"I shall never see his cursed face again. I swear I never shall!"

"I say, you poor trembling idiot, that you are going back to Peter Quince and give him a message for me."

"It is an honor worth more than gold to poor Juan Garien."

"Very good! Go back to this Peter Quince and tell him that I have let him live the first time because he was young. But that the second time I come to him I shall surely kill him."

"I shall tell him that, señor. Be sure that I shall spend every one of your words on him, as if it were precious gold!"

"And tell him that if he leaves the country at once and rides on farther south, all is well. I shall not trouble him.

He is young, and young men are apt to make mistakes. Tell him this, and then bid him ride fast and hard. Tell him that El Tigre has spoken!"

"I shall remember every word. I shall sing them in my mind all the way I run back, so that I shall not forget!"

"That is good, Juan. Take this!" And he closed the gold into the hand of the poor peon.

"Now tell me," said El Tigre, "what message was sent with you?"

"Merely foolish words."

"You ran seven miles at full speed to deliver those foolish words. What are they, Juan Garien?"

"It would wither my tongue to speak them!"

"I'll tell you, blockhead, that I'll wring your neck unless you speak out freely and clearly!"

Juan dropped into the position of the greatest safety— that is to say, he fell upon his knees. "He bade me go to you—he threatened me with terrible death unless I sent the message to El Tigre, though I prayed him—"

"Very well, come to the words!"

"He ordered me to tell you—but I cannot speak it, señor."

"Come!"

"He said that he would come to hunt you, El Tigre!"

"Ah?"

"And that when he caught you he would stretch your hide upon the rocks!"

"This is very good."

"And that he would feed your body to coyotes and buzzards! In the name of mercy, señor, the words are his, not mine!"

"I believe it," said El Tigre. "And so, stand up!"

The latter rose.

"Go back to the foolish boy and tell him that I would have let him go free if I could, but that since he had insulted me, he must die."

"I shall tell him those words, El Tigre."

"Quickly!"

Juan Garien disappeared. He fled so fast that in a twinkling he was up the slope and out of view beyond the crest. But El Tigre stood for a long time in the deepest thought. At last Pedro Rincon stole away and came back leading the great chestnut horse. Even then, when Pedro spoke, there was no answer from the outlaw.

"They will come on your trail, El Tigre," said the old man at length.

There was no answer.

"They may come suddenly, señor."

Still El Tigre was silent.

"And when they come, though El Tigre may be gone, the old man still will be here."

At this the bandit roused himself at last and laid a hand on the shoulder of Rincon. "We go at once," he said. "Saddle your horse and come with me."

Pedro Rincon turned, but he was called back by El Tigre.

"But stay where you are—stay here in the hut, Pedro. A man who is brave enough to send a challenge to El Tigre is too brave to attack an old man. This fellow is brave, Pedro, and there is more danger in him than in twenty rats like Juan Garien!"

16. WAITING FOR EL TIGRE

FOR THREE miles Juan Garien ran so fast that his eyes turned up in his head, and his knees became like water, refusing to bear him up. He slowed to a jog, but even then he stared behind him over his shoulder to watch the coming danger. Finally his wind came back to him, and Juan went on. As he neared the village, his courage was somewhat restored. Still it was a dusty and humbled figure that reached Peter Quince at last.

"You gave the message?"

"To El Tigre himself!" cried Juan Garien.

He caught his breath. It seemed impossible that he, with his own lips, had spoken to the terrible man; that with his own eyes he had beheld the destroyer.

"To El Tigre?" murmured Peter, and he saw so much excitement in the face of the other that he knew the fellow was speaking the truth.

"To El Tigre himself I spoke!"

"And what did you say then?"

"He was eating dinner when I came to him."

"Dinner at this hour in the morning?"

"He only eats once a day, señor."

"Is that true?"

"Every child knows that it is true of El Tigre. He was eating, I say, when I came up to him."

"What was he eating, Juan?"

"Roasted beef—and garlic!"

"At this time of the day? Whatever else he may be, he has a mighty stomach!"

"If there is no fire near he eats the beef raw."

"Really, Juan?"

"Really, señor."

Peter Quince swallowed his smile. There was such a deal of credulity and deceit in Juan that it was difficult to tell where he was lying, or had been lied to.

"Very well then. You came upon El Tigre eating raw beef."

"It was cooked meat with garlic!"

"You rogue!" shouted Peter. "Has there been time for him to get to that place and have a roast cooked since he left the village here?"

"Nevertheless," murmured Juan, "it was as I have said. He looked up to me when I stood before him. 'Why have you come so late?' says he to me."

"Very glad to see you then, Juan?"

"Very, señor. He asked me why I had not come before. 'But why,' said I, 'should I have come?'

" 'Because I have always room for brave men near me,' says El Tigre.

" 'You are kind,' says I.

" 'I am only wise,' said he. 'I know a man of worth—and therefore, I know you, Juan Garien.' "

"A polite bandit," said Peter Quince.

"I tell you only his very words, señor."

"Why, Juan, I know perfectly well that nothing could make you lie."

"Nothing, señor."

"But continue."

" 'I shall make you a rich man in my service, Juan,'

says he. 'Señor El Tigre,' says I, 'it is too late. I am serving a man who is your enemy.' At this he claps his hand to his heart. 'I have lost you then, Juan?' 'You have!'

" 'I see black days before me,' said El Tigre. 'Continue! Who is this man?'

" 'One who says that he will stretch your hide on the rocks and feed you to buzzards and coyotes!'

"He jumped up and began to curse. 'Señor,' I said, as cool as this, 'curses will not help you. My master is resolved to have your blood!'

" 'I shall kill him,' said El Tigre. 'Go back and tell him that I shall come instantly to kill him!'

"And yet, señor, you see that he has not come. But I could see it in his eye: 'If the servant is not afraid of me, what will the master be like?' He is beginning to be frightened, señor. In truth, he is!"

"I see how it will be," said Peter Quince. "I shall sit at home at ease and send you out to do my fighting for me. All will be well! When El Tigre comes, I shall send you to face him."

The glance of Juan wandered a little.

"I am yours to command, señor."

"After the command of Monterey?"

"You have seen my confession."

"Juan, stand straight and look me in the eye."

It was done.

"Confess: You were behind the deviltry of throwing that knife into the room of poor Señor Avery last night."

"Señor—knife—thrown! I cannot tell what is meant!"

"You are an expert and convincing liar. Nevertheless—"

"Upon my honor—"

"And you had nothing to do with the cutting of the letters into the wood?"

"Nothing, señor. What letters?"

"You should have asked that first. However, I haven't the time to corner such a slippery rascal. What does Monterey wish with me?"

"He wished only to see you."

"He honors me. Have you guessed at his reason, Juan?"

"I have."

"What is it?"

"I dare not put words into his mouth, señor."

He became instantly so sober and grave that Peter saw it was useless to try to obtain anything from him concerning his employer.

"And if I go to see him, what surety have I that he'll deal fairly with me?"

"The proof, señor, that the letter was cut out from the sill of your window and the floor of your hall."

"You confess that you know of it?"

"I have been told."

"Tell me then, Juan, why so many of your people serve Monterey?"

"Because he is kind."

"Ah?"

"And generous and true. If I work for him today and go sick tomorrow, I am taken care of for the rest of my life till I die. His servants are his children. He cares for them as if he were caring for himself. And that is what he says. When a cruel man once asked him why he spent so much money on his servants he said: 'They are part of me. They are my hands, my feet, my ears and my eyes. Those who cook my food, labor in my fields, dig in my garden, build my houses, dig my ditches, are all parts of me. Do you understand?' "

"I find it hard to follow," said Peter, "but it sounds like a pretty idea."

"It is very true," said the other.

"Do you personally think that Señor Monterey would leave me unharmed if I were in his power?"

"I cannot think for him. But if I were he, I should not touch a man who came to me on trust."

"But you are not Señor Monterey."

"I swear to you that he is in every way a much better man than I!"

Again Peter laughed and was disarmed by this perfect naïveté.

"Juan," he said, "get ready to guide me to his house. I go to him at once, as soon as I have met with this loud-talking El Tigre."

"Until when?"

"Until El Tigre comes!"

"The señor does not think of meeting him?"

"I shall never rest until I have him. And to begin with, I shall wait here until noon to see if this man-eater comes. No, better than that—I shall leave the town and wait for him among the hills."

"Ah, he would swoop down like an eagle upon a lamb!"

"He'll find me tough meat, Juan Garien. Besides, he may not even know that I'm waiting for him, eh?"

"He knows all things quickly. He has an eye everywhere. My own brother may be one of El Tigre's men. How shall I know? He may buy my secrets from my mother!" And poor Juan turned up his eyes in terror.

"How have you the courage to stand against him then?" asked Peter curiously.

"Señor Monterey pays much money!"

That was the secret. "Well," said Peter Quince, "look out yonder to that flat-topped hill."

"I see it well."

"I shall wait half the day there for El Tigre."

"Señor! No!"

"Spread the news, Juan. That's my final word."

And this was how the strangest and, from a certain aspect, the most foolish day of Peter's life was spent. He rode, as he had promised, straight to the hill, and there he waited. The sun climbed high. On neighboring hills here and yonder he saw figures of men working up to a position from which they could see with advantage. The noon declined into the afternoon. He lay down in the sun, put his head on his saddle, and went to sleep. When he awakened, the evening was beginning, and the sun was down. He had made up with a vengeance for his broken slumbers of the night before, but there was no sign to show that El Tigre had come. He stood up, stretched himself and looked about him. And he saw scores of men and women and children still waiting in the distance, spellbound, soundless.

He climbed into his saddle and rode back to the village. And behind him scurried the crowd and began to clatter and chatter, as they ran. At the tavern he found Juan Garien. The fellow was gray with wonder and fear.

"Where is your swooping eagle—where is El Tigre, Juan?"

"Señor, I cannot even speak!"

17. A PANTHER AND A BEAR

AND THE VILLAGE was not the only place where there was silence and wonder, as the dusk came on. Five minutes after Peter left the town to go out and wait for the bandit, a runner slipped away on the opposite side of the town, wove among the hills until he had cut around to the west, and settled to a steady jog. He was making for El Tigre, but how could he have known where to find the man? That was apparently settled in his mind by the sight of two columns of smoke, two thin columns which almost melted into the haze of sky-blue. They burned far away to the north of the town, but by them the runner headed to the west. He worked for two hours at a pace which would have strained a good horse. Then he came on his quarry. No doubt he had been seen in the distance and had been allowed to come in simply because he was known to be a friend. But, dodging through the rocks, he came upon a little opening, where a party of a dozen were lounging in the shadows.

He had been struggling up sharp slopes for two hours; he had been running for two hours, on fire with exciting news; but the moment he saw the man to whom the news was to be delivered, he slowed his pace to a walk, sobered his labor-drawn face to an expression of indifference and, appropriating to himself the shady side of a large boulder, he dropped down cross-legged, and began to manufacture a cigarette.

While he made the smoke and lighted it, no one addressed him, nor for another minute, while the smoke coiled thin and small above his head. But at length he was offered a canteen. His dark eyes flashed a glance of thanks. He tilted the canteen, and yet he took only a few swallows. The long race and the dust and the heat, together with the last irritation of tobacco smoke, had given him such a thirst that he could easily have drained the canteen twice over, but pride kept him from exposing his necessity. The few swallows moistened his throat, made it easier to breathe, and took the knife-edge from his thirst.

But here a tall and slender fellow, built like a dancer, for agility and grace, and dressed in a jacket covered with gold braid and trousers brilliant with silver conchos, stepped up to the newcomer. It was the lieutenant of El Tigre. It was no other than "Guillermo Suave," or William the Soft. And Guillermo retained carefully the velvet touch and saved the harsh word for the harsh moment. He had been known to shriek and sing and weep in the hysteria of a battle, for he fought like a madman or a drunkard; but ordinarily his manner was as gentle as the manner of a girl. He was, in fact, more dreaded than El Tigre himself, and for his cruelty he was famous over the length and the breadth of the barren mountains.

"And so," he said, as he leaned an elbow on the edge of the rock and smiled down at the runner, "you have been in trouble again and come for help?"

"Not so, señor!" cried the runner.

"No," murmured Guillermo, and his lifted brows and faint smile assured the others that he had been merely drawing out the messenger.

"I have come with great news for El Tigre!"

"Then that is good!"

No one in the sprawling circle stirred to hear the news the better—not even El Tigre.

"Sometimes even El Tigre may go hungry because he finds it hard to get fat deer?" grinned the runner.

"That might be," nodded Guillermo.

"But no more hunger shall come to him."

"Ah?"

"I have said it! Men are going mad. They are throwing themselves into the stretch of his claws."

"What is this then?"

"A man waits on the hill near the city for the coming of El Tigre!"

"Does he? He *waits* for El Tigre?"

Every member of the crew sat up now. Their ages were from fifteen to sixty; the nationalities were from dark to light; the costumes were predominantly Mexican, but with many variations. There were faces smooth-shaven and bearded; there were blue eyes and black; but the country had swallowed their differences and made them all of one type. Dangers and hard riding and mountain silences had pressed one stamp upon them all. They waited in the shadows for the concluding part of the riddle of the messenger.

"He waits!" cried the runner. "And there are hundreds of others in the distance, knowing that El Tigre will come down, and they are hungry to see him make a kill in the broad daylight."

"What manner of madman is this?" asked Guillermo, when the muttering of the astonished crew died away.

"A gringo."

Ranjel Verial rose to his feet. If Guillermo was the panther of the crew, Ranjel was the bear. He had a little head, set between shoulders plumped and padded with muscle. And he had long arms, fat with muscle, also. He looked extremely clumsy, and yet he was as fast as an animal. And there is no human speed which can equal the deftness of a wild beast. Ranjel Verial was wild. There was only one thing which kept him from being as great and as famous a warrior as El Tigre himself, and that was the size of his little round black eyes. They spoke of the cramped brain within. Indeed, if he could have freed himself from the burden of awe which weighed him down, there was no reason why Ranjel Verial could not have destroyed even El Tigre. But El Tigre crushed him with his assurance and with a sense of some mysterious control. If El Tigre so much as raised his voice, a tremor of uneasiness passed through the body of Ranjel.

Now, however, he heard of ordinary game walking abroad and giving challenges, and his face and throat swelled with anger and eagerness. He could not keep his fingers from touching the butt of his revolver and then passing on to his knife haft. El Tigre himself sat up.

"I can tell you the name of this man," he said.

There was another exclamation.

"Can you read?" asked El Tigre.

"I cannot."

"This is his name." And El Tigre scrawled in the sand: "Peter Quince."

He said aloud: "Describe him then."

"He is pale, señor."

"And his eyes?"

"They are blue."

"And his hair?"

"Yellow gold!"

"Like a girl!" laughed Ranjel Verial.

"Bah!" cried El Tigre, "you speak like a fool, Ranjel!"

All were dumb with amazement. If an enemy was not to be abused freely, what then?

"I should go down to have a little talk with him then," said Ranjel, "if he were not calling for El Tigre first!"

"I am not going!"

It was another thunderclap. His followers stared at one another.

"Let me go," put in Ranjel.

"He would cut you to pieces."

"I'll bring back his ears. Even if El Tigre fears him—"

There was a dull roar from the leader.

"Fears?" he thundered. "Who asks if I fear any man?"

Ranjel shrank. "A thousand pardons!" he muttered.

"Look here!" called El Tigre, and he rose to his feet in his turn. He was very tall indeed, even among those stalwarts. And his pale eyes flashed across their faces. They shrank from him, as though he were announcing in so many words that he had read their suspicions of his fear when he failed to answer the challenge of the gringo.

"Guillermo!" he commanded. "What have I written? What is the name of the gringo?"

"Peter Quince," answered Guillermo.

There was a little breath of wonder from the others. For the messenger had cried instantly in terror and astonishment: "Nothing is hidden from the eye of El Tigre! It is true indeed. The name of the man is Peter Quince!"

"And I tell all my good friends to keep away from him," said El Tigre. "There is only one man now breathing who can face him and beat him, and that man is I! Remember

what I have said, Ranjel Verial! If you hunt him down,
he'll cut you to bits!"

He turned to the messenger.

"Although I knew all of these things," he said, "yet I
am pleased that you have come to me at once. Here is
something for you, and if ever there is trouble in your
family, I shall remember you!"

He took from his pocket a thick wallet and opened it.
It was gorged to the clasps with thickly wadded bills.
From that dense sheaf he selected one of a large denom-
ination and passed it to the gaping runner.

"Adios!" said El Tigre and the messenger backed from
his presence, as if from before the face of a king.

He left behind him, however, the first wound for the
fair fame of El Tigre. Before this day it could never have
been said that the leader had drawn back from conflict
with any man. But now, no matter for what good reason
he had refused a fight, the reserved look in every eye
meant only one thing—his followers were dreaming of the
great day to come, when even El Tigre must grow old or
careless and fall. And when that happened, each man was
telling himself that he was big enough to step into the shoes
of the leader.

Particularly these thoughts grew in the brain of Ranjel
Verial. And, as he walked apart from the others a little
later, his purpose grew firm. Suppose that he should go
down to face the man who had been shunned by the
leader? Suppose that in battle he should crush this gringo
—might not his companions in the band think something
and say something when he returned in glory?

The mind of Ranjel Verial moved slowly, but in the mid-
afternoon he reached a determination, and when the evening began to descend he was missed from the camp.
News of it was brought to El Tigre, who merely
shrugged.

"He has gone to be killed. I should have been sorry a
month ago, but since then Ranjel has become too fat to
be useful, so let it be!" And he rolled another cigarette.

18. DON PETER SHOOTS

IN A CORNER of the kitchen sat Peter Quince. The reason of his being there was a dark-eyed beauty of seventeen who hurried busily from one place to another, though the work which she did with her hands was far less effective than that which she accomplished with her glances. Sometimes she caught up the round grass broom and swept the hard-packed dirt floor, though this was already clean beyond imagination; sometimes she fed the fire, which burned in a chimney inside a half circular opening of great size, and raised perhaps three feet from the ground; and sometimes she gave her attention to the turning of the spit, on which there was browning a kid, skinned and drawn, and with the head and feet cut off.

The fat hissed and spat back into the fire, and a delicious odor filled the room, together with a smoke which rolled lazily toward the ceiling, or licked out through the door, the upper half, or ventanna, of which was thrown open. In fact, it was the only window to air the big kitchen. The major portion of the work was being accomplished by the sturdy old moza whose brown hands moved slowly, but with purpose. Young Rosa was there to serve her apprenticeship in this important phase of housewifery, but this evening was a wasted season.

How else could it have been? The strange and wonderful man who defied and challenged El Tigre, and who had lived to tell of it afterward, had not only chosen her among all the girls of the village, but he had so far signified his preference that he was actually sitting in the kitchen with her! As a matter of fact, Rosa did not know whether to be more happy or more scornful with a man who so far stooped beneath his dignity as actually to step into the smoke of a kitchen. But the gringo was either beneath or above personal dignity. He had stood at the open ventanna of the door and sung to her, thrumming on a guitar for an accompaniment. And now he sat in a corner of the kitchen and talked to her, with the guitar across his knees, and from which he occasionally struck out a lively or a plaintive air.

Both his auditors listened, pleased.

Even her mother, though she was rigid enough in the overseeing of her daughter's conduct, could not frown upon a conversation with so distinguished a warrior. Perhaps she was only delighted to see that the beauty of her daughter could bring a hero into a kitchen! There would be talk about this on the morrow, but it was not hard for her to guess that her daughter would be only the more prized by her lover, the son of the well-to-do butcher, who walked down the street of the village every morning with a long pole over his shoulder, and from the end of the pole strings of meat depending, and shouting, as he walked: *"Carne! Carne!"* He might be angry when he heard how the gringo had been entertained; but doubtless he would be only flattered in the end to think that his fiancée had such attractions.

In the meantime, the conversation between the two consisted almost entirely of the most meaningless banalities, interspersed with silences of formidable dimensions, only disturbed when Peter Quince touched out an air on the guitar. These pauses disturbed, or seemed to disturb, Rosa.

"You are thinking, señor," she said presently.

"Yes," he answered.

"You are thinking of someone far away."

"Yes."

"It is a lady."

"Yes."

He watched with pleasure, while the shadow deepened on her face.

"I have been remembering the hands of all the women I have ever known."

"Ah!"

It was a pretty thing to watch the shadow half lift and see her poised in expectancy for the compliment, none the less delightful for being half expected.

"And I can remember not one, Rosa, with hands as lovely as yours."

"Señor! But it is to those other ladies you are talking with your music."

For even then, as they spoke, his fingers were going lightly, lightly, over the strings.

"However, of that you can never be sure, Rosa."

She blinked at him, quite amazed at such frankness. Such was not the habit of the wooers to whom she was accustomed. Then, gradually, she smiled again, and her great eyes softened on him.

"Of this," she said, "I can never be sure. And there have been so many ladies, señor?"

"I have always worshipped beauty from a distance," said Peter Quince.

"Shall I believe that?"

"If you will," said Peter, and they laughed together.

A one-eyed man with a hideous face appeared at the window. His hat came off. His grin was fastened appealingly upon Rosa.

"May you marry wealth and have many sons, señorita."

"Thief!" cried Rosa, whirling on him. "Have you forgotten how you were whipped out of town last month?"

"Hunger makes one forget many things."

"You are a fool then!"

"There is so much to eat in your house—one morsel wouldn't be missed!"

"Not a scrap big enough to keep a rat alive!"

Peter wondered at her vindictiveness, and no doubt the beggar understood the expression of his face.

"Señor," he said, "I am starving!"

"The devil!" muttered Peter Quince. Taking a half-dollar from his pocket, he spun it toward the window and the one-eyed face. But the slender round arm of Rosa darted out. The winking coin was snatched out of the air.

"I tell you, I *know* that man, and he is bad, bad, bad!" cried Rosa, and she dropped the half-dollar into her pocket.

"May the wrinkles come early!" said the beggar.

"You rat eater!" snarled the lovely Rosa. And she poised a cup full of boiling grease.

The beggar dodged out of sight and was apparently so little affected by this cruel indifference to the wants of his stomach that he began to whistle an air in a shrill key.

"Listen!" said Rosa. "You see what he is? He is the most shameless beggar and the worst rascal in Mexico! There are some who say that he serves El Tigre, but I know that El Tigre is too great to use such a dog!"

"Listen!" murmured Peter Quince. "That is a strange air he is whistling. It is sharp enough to travel a mile; and there is not a great deal of tune to it."

"What do you mean?" asked Rosa. "He probably knows no other song. You know that very bad people all hate music! It's like so much poison to them."

"Really?" said Peter, swallowing his smile. "But at least there is enough strength to that whistle to make it serve as a signal—eh?"

Rosa turned and looked sharply at him.

"Signal?" she said.

"It is nothing," said Peter, and he began to thrum at the guitar and sing in a voice which could hardly pass the walls of the kitchen a love song, the words of which must have been unknown to Rosa, but the sound of the singing made her head tilt from side to side, like a heavy blossom in a lazy wind of June.

At the same time, however, he turned his chair more directly toward the ventanna and twisted a little in his chair, a maneuver which exposed the butt of his revolver more readily to his fingers. The whistle of the beggar in the meantime had died into the distance, and then ceased. Peter raised his voice until it rang.

"How beautiful!" cried Rosa. And she was drawn closer to him. She stood at last just beside his chair, gazing down at him, dwelling on the glimmering yellow of his hair, as though it were metal gold indeed. "While you sing," she said, "the moza will not come in for fear of stopping your song. You must not dare to stop singing, Don Peter!"

And, as she warned him with one lifted finger, she leaned as swiftly as a bird stoops, and her warm lips brushed his forehead. The song of Peter Quince trembled like a candle flame when a draft shakes it, but the singing did not quite die out. The song rose again. He was singing straight to the eyes of Rosa, half bending above him.

"If you stop singing!" she cried again. "If you stop, the moza will come again! You dare not stop, Don Peter!"

And she leaned again; but when she straightened, it seemed to Peter Quince that he had made out a vague shadow standing at the door of the kitchen, his shoulders showing big and broad outside the ventanna. It had been only a glimpse, as the arm of Rosa stirred, but it made the right hand of Peter stop thrumming the strings and descend smoothly to the butt of his revolver. He raised his voice, as though to make up for the lack of accompaniment. Then, with a sweep of his left arm, he thrust Rosa aside and whipped up the revolver.

He fired not an instant too soon. For the big man outside the door had stood there with a revolver leveled, the barrel gleaming brightly against the black of the mask which covered his features. His own bullet hummed just over the head of Peter; then he was driven back by the shock of an unseen hand and fell from sight.

The scream of Rosa ran like a saw-edge through the echoes of the shots, and she clung to Peter as he started for the door.

"He's only pretending!" she cried. "He's waiting to kill you there—it's Ranjel Verial—it's Ranjel Verial!"

"Then he's waiting," said Peter, "with a bullet hole through his heart."

Peter freed himself from her clinging hands and went forward, just as the door, which opened into the interior of the house, was knocked open, and a flood of people spilled into the kitchen. They reached the outer door at the heels of Peter Quince and, leaning out, they found themselves staring down at a mighty form whose arms were outspread and from whose face the mask had been torn by his own hands, as he gasped for breath in the death struggle. It was Ranjel Verial, and he was dead.

Who had done it? Was it possible that Verial was no longer living? Was it, indeed, true that those brilliant, staring eyes saw nothing? Peter Quince stared down at the face in wonder, for, though he had fought and had killed before, he had never before felt the full miracle of a life current stopped and turned into a wide pool of silence. He could hear Rosa explaining the doughty deed in the background, with a few necessary alterations.

"I heard a sound that was like no sound at all behind me," she was saying, "and was afraid. I was as cold in my blood as though I had stepped into the middle of winter. I turned around, and there I saw a masked face at the ventanna and a pair of thick shoulders. I knew it was Ranjel Verial. I had never seen him before, but I knew it was he. I had heard him described too often. His arms are like the two forelegs of a puma, someone had said. And that was what I thought of, as I looked at him.

"He had a gun raised, and, just as he turned, he dropped the gun, and I screamed. I tell you, señores, that Don Peter was sitting yonder in that chair playing on the guitar and singing. Why, you all heard him singing up to the last moment.

"Señores, he saw the danger only through my scream, but he whirled in the chair, spun a revolver into his hand, and fired—all this, señores, while the terrible Verial was dropping his gun on the mark! But Verial was killed. I thought for an instant that it must have been a flash of lightning from heaven that struck him down. I was so sure that Don Peter was no better than a dead man!"

19.   MUTE TESTIMONY

What Peter had done he felt had been lucky and re- markable enough without the tale of Rosa to turn his work into a miracle. But she established him, by the undeniable evidence of an eyewitness, as one who, though taken by surprise, had destroyed a terrible enemy by no more than a casual gesture. A sudden murmur ran through the crowd of listeners.

"Then this is why El Tigre did not come to meet him! He was truly afraid of him! He was afraid! El Tigre was afraid and sent Verial to do the murder!"

It looked exceedingly like it even to Peter, though when he recalled the face of the huge horseman who had shot at him in the patio of the tavern, it did not seem that there could possibly be the slightest room for fear in the soul of such a man. But, in the meantime, he found himself regarded as a hero by the entire town. Men and women began to look at him in reverence. Even Rosa, as though she were beginning to be convinced by the frequent repetition of her own tale, no longer regarded him as an amiable equal, but as a renowned destroyer.

When he retired to his room in the tavern that night, there was a tap at his door, and it was opened upon the face of Juan Garien. That nimble-tongued rascal had forgotten his usual dashing air for the moment.

"Is it true?" was all he could stammer. "Is it true?"

"Come inside, Juan," said Peter, amused. "Is what true?"

"Have you done still another thing today?" gasped Juan.

"What other thing, Juan?"

"The killing of Ranjel Verial!"

"Oh, you refer to that?"

Upon the lips of Juan appeared the faintest of smiles, as though acknowledging that there was a jest in the tone of Peter, but at the same time having neither time nor inclination to pursue trivial affairs.

"I refer to that. In the name of heaven, señor, do you kill a Verial every day?"

"Only on holidays, Juan."

"But was it done as the girl said—when you were taken by surprise—when your back was turned?"

"You may believe that if you please."

"But should I believe it? Only tell me one thing, señor—"

"A thousand things, if you wish."

"Was his gun drawn before yours?"

"It was, Juan."

Juan crossed himself.

"It is a marvelous thing to see that you are still living, señor. If it had been any other man than Verial—"

"Well?"

"But tell me before I die of curiosity—was it really from fear that El Tigre stayed away from you today?"

"I have no desire to read the mind of El Tigre," said Peter Quince, "but when I meet the scoundrel I intend to tie him to a cactus and horsewhip him!"

To this absurd jest, to the surprise of Peter, Juan Garien did not reply with laughter, nor even with a smile. Instead, his eyes opened wider, and he nodded at Peter, as though to declare his utter conviction that the thing must be exactly as he had stated.

"Well," said Juan Garien, "then I must give you this letter."

He accordingly took from an inner pocket a fold of leather, which evidently served him as a wallet, and from this, with the greatest care, he extracted an envelope which he handed to Peter. It was of white and heavy paper and it was as unstained as though it had not yet been under the hand of a writer. The name of Peter Quince was inscribed upon it in a hand of wonderful delicacy. There was no stamp in the corner.

"This," said Peter, "comes from whom?"

"You will find the name of the writer within, señor. I am not permitted to speak of that subject."

So Peter examined the face of the rascal again with great circumspection. Then he opened the note. He read as follows:

Tuesday in the morning. From Casa Monterey.

To Señor Don Peter Quince.

"How absurd are these titles," thought Peter, "in front of a name like mine!"

"My dear Señor Quince," began the body of the letter, "I have today heard astonishing tidings concerning you. They are no other than that, having first in vain defied and awaited the coming of the celebrated El Tigre, you were treacherously attacked, and by no other person than the infamous Ranjel Verial. I have heard also that, though taken by surprise, you have killed this bandit. Now, having only paused to ascertain that this is actually true, I am placing this letter in your hand.

"You will have heard of me before through our mutual friend, the clever young engineer, Martin Avery; but I assure you that, in spite of the considerable length at which he discussed me with you, you will find that the report he gave of me was erroneous in a great degree. If you wonder why I begin a letter to a man whom I have not yet seen face to face, with personalities, you must understand that I have resolved to bring you to my house as my guest.

"And lest you should be deterred from coming by considering that men do not invite strangers to their houses, I may tell you that after what you have done today, you and I cannot continue as strangers. We need one another. If you will come to me, I shall inform you in full of how we can and must be of use to one another. Señor, I may step beyond the limits of ordinary prudence and declare to you that a great calamity is threatening me, and that it is threatening you, also, and that we alone can be of assistance to one another in the crisis. Come to me and let me describe to you our mutual peril. Or, if you doubt the truth of what I have told you, remain where you are and receive the first proofs of your danger.

"As for the tales which you have heard from Martin Avery, I shall not deny the facts, as he has spoken them; and Señor Avery is incapable, I believe, of deliberately telling an untruth. Nevertheless, no matter of how sensitive a nature, a weakling cannot comprehend the mind and the motives of the strong man. And that circumstantial evidence may often point to false conclusions, I need hardly suggest to you, since your experience with Joseph Paul.

"In the meantime, I shall expect your answer whenever you have found the time to make up your mind. There is no immediate haste.

"In case you decide to visit me, you may trust yourself for guidance to the hands of Juan Garien, who is fully as clever as you think him and much more honest.

"I remain your humble and obedient servant,
                                        Felipe Monterey."

What Peter Quince first did, as he ran his eye over the signature, was to glance sharply up to the face of the young Mexican. But the eye of the latter was as open as the door of a barn, and invited his searching look to enter and see all that was within his mind. Then Peter considered the manuscript again. He felt that he had in his hand the letter of a most forward and honest man, or else the epistle of an errant charlatan, and not too clever a one at that. Nine-tenths of what was written in the letter might well be composed simply to impress him and dispose him toward the writer. But in the other tenth there was an air of earnestness which could not be avoided.

"Juan," he said suddenly, "where has Señor Monterey been staying near the town?"

"Near the town?"

"When he wrote this letter."

"He was not near the town."

"How far away?"

"About forty miles—in the Casa Monterey, señor."

Peter Quince smiled.

"I am the simplest fellow in the world," he said. "I will willingly believe the most absurd fables and follies; but you don't expect to convince me that the news of the killing of Ranjel Verial—in the three or four hours since he was killed—has traveled forty miles through the mountains, reached Casa Monterey, and that this letter has been written by him and dispatched—and all in the space of three hours and a half at the most; that this distance of eighty miles through rough country has been traveled—"

"I cannot explain, señor, but you have the letter in your own hand."

"What rascality is beneath all this?"

"Rascality?"

"Sit down again, Juan, and roll another cigarette. I am not through with you!"

He spoke the last a little grimly, and there was an instant change in Juan. His face remained immobile, good actor that he was, but he straightened a little and flashed a single glance at the window. Then, as though he realized that he was helpless, he sank into the chair and looked steadily upon his host. An instant later he was deliberately rolling the cigarette. He lighted it with admirable steadiness, and blew the smoke at the ceiling, and yet Peter Quince knew that the fellow was all the time in the throes of the most mortal terror.

"I am at your command," he said mildly.

"I must have the truth, Juan."

"As far as I know—the absolute truth."

"Where did you get this letter?"

"It was thrown through the window of my house and fell into my lap."

"Come, come, Juan! Do you expect me to believe such a fairy tale as this?"

"Upon my honor, it is just as I say."

"You did not see the face of the man who threw the letter in?"

"No, señor."

"Then his tracks are covered, I suppose?"

"He was on horseback. He threw in the letter. I saw only his bare hand, as it flashed away. He called one word and was gone."

"What was the word?"

"Monterey."

"Of course, that would be it." And he smiled upon Juan Garien, but the latter showed only desire to be believed. You admit that this is absurd, Juan?"

"There are many things about Señor Monterey which are absurd," said Juan gravely.

"What are a few to match this?"

"I cannot talk of him."

There was a dignity about the demeanor of Juan at this juncture that made Peter Quince half ashamed of his querulous questionings.

"Frankly, what do you think that I should do, Juan?"

"What Señor Monterey commands you to do."

"Commands?"

A faint smile disturbed the lips of Juan. "Do you think that you are above obeying the commands of Monterey?"

"Or of any other man."

Juan leaned back in his chair and shrugged his shoulders. "It is not for me to teach you wisdom, señor!"

"I'll see him singing in the fire of the damned," said Peter with violence. "He can't humbug me into dancing to his music."

Juan Garien rose. His lips were trembling with fear, though his gesture was one of only mild deprecation. "You are speaking of Señor Monterey?" he suggested.

"Who else?"

"Señor, if you are a wise man, you will not linger long in this country!"

"Bah!" said Peter Quince. "First your El Tigre threatens me, and now this Monterey. They are no more than the wind to me. Go tell this parlor magician what I've said!"

"You are very brave," said Juan, but he left the other half of his sentence unspoken. He turned to the door and was gone.

"One more thing," cried Peter, remembering. "Tell him when—"

He had opened the door to call back Garien, but, as the door swung wide, something glinted before the eyes of Peter, something which hissed faintly and touched his forehead like fire. It struck heavily against the wooden trim of the door, and Peter found himself looking at a heavy knife with a long, straight blade, just such a knife as that which he had seen fixed as a warning in the wall above the head of Martin Avery.

But this was no warning. The sting of the sharp edge was still biting at his flesh, and Peter Quince went mad with fighting fury. Usually, in battle, he was the personification of coolness, like the majority of those who depend upon their adroitness rather than sheer strength to win their assaults at arms. But the caution had left Peter now. He raced down the hall like a tiger, whipped around the elbow turn and saw nothing before him!

He raced on. He came to the view of the head of the stairs, and there he saw his man—there was Juan Garien in the very act of descending!

"Señor!" cried Juan, stepping back with an upraised hand of amazement.

Straight on came Peter Quince, as fast as a wolf runs as it gathers for the spring and the kill. His left fist flashed past the hand of the other, and Garien went down. Imagine a hundred and sixty pounds of compact weight placed all behind a small, iron-hard fist. Imagine that fist traveling like an arrow just loosed from the bow. And then it is easy to understand what happened to Juan Garien. He left his feet, turned in the air, crashed heavily upon his back and rolled with violence against the wall. Peter Quince picked him up by the hair of his head, took him by the throat and jammed his head against the wall again.

"You dirty cutthroat! You black-livered murderer!"

cried Peter, forgetting his Spanish in the emergency and lapsing into vigorous Western English.

Then he saw that, though the eyes of Juan were partially open, they were entirely devoid of intelligence; his whole body was limp, and the wits of Juan were in a far country gathering wool. So Peter let him slump to the floor, where he sat in a loose heap, with his head sagging to one side, like one of Homer's warriors after the sword had done its work. Peter looked his man over with a rage which gradually passed into contempt. He was beginning to regret his fury, moreover, and to tell himself what might have happened had he so blindly attacked a foeman more worthy of his steel, when he noted the belt of Juan Garien and saw there the hilt of a knife. Peter Quince stared wildly. For here was mute testimony that Garien had not thrown the knife which so narrowly missed his head. If Juan had not, then who was the guilty man? Had Juan Garien told some other person of the result of the interview and given him an order to assassinate? No, Juan had not had the time, it seemed, to talk to anyone. It could only be explained that their conversation had been overheard, and that this was the result of the eavesdropping.

The sum total, from one side of the question, was that he had more enemies, and Monterey had more agents, than he knew anything about. The other conclusion was certainly that he had just knocked down an innocent man. He did not know which was the more disagreeable conclusion. But now Juan was opening his eyes and sighing. So Peter slipped an arm under the shoulders of the fallen man and lifted him up. He led him back to the room they had just left, and deposited him gently in a chair. Then Juan looked up, shook his head, muttered an indistinguishable thing, and started out of his chair. Peter, expecting either a bullet or the end of a knife at his ribs, recoiled a pace.

"Juan," he said, "I acted too quickly. I am a thousand times sorry!"

"So, señor, is my jaw!"

And, to the amazement of Peter, Juan laid a hand on his chin and laughed heartily. He added an instant later: "If anyone had seen that, I should, of course, murder

you, Señor Quince. But, since no one saw, I have only to
say that your fist is like an iron club. Why do you wear a
gun?"

Such good-humor melted the last of Peter's unwilling-
ness under the double sum of curiosity and regret for what
had just passed.

"Juan," he said, "this is the argument that convinces me
your master must be an honest man. If you are ready,
we'll start tonight for the Casa Monterey."

His tone was firm.

Juan Garien clapped his hands like a child.

"For this," he said, "I would stand to be knocked down
again! When I bring you, I shall be promoted!"

"To what?" asked Peter Quince.

"To the rank above me," said Juan Garien, still rubbing the spot where the knuckles of Peter had bruised
the flesh.

20. EN ROUTE

THEY STARTED on the ride at once. Juan climbed into the
saddle, which was already on the back of a fine animal,
and Peter saddled Bad Luck. The gray horse was rejuven-
ated by the long rest and the heavy feeding. His sides
had rounded, the painful straight line of his gaunt belly
had disappeared, and the neck of the stallion was curving
proudly again. He was not only rested, but he was fretting
for work, and the neighing and pawing he set up when he
saw the master was a sufficient evidence of that.

So the two horsemen swung away at a canter which
lasted until the hills began to pitch up before them. Then
they pulled back to a jog-trot, and in this pace they continued through the greater part of the journey. But it was
stiff work for the horses, laboring up steep inclines, or
pitching down dark slopes, or weaving among the boulders and the sharp rocks up the throat of some twisted
ravine. Before they had covered the thirty or forty miles
of their trip the dawn had come and touched the sky

with rose, the rose had turned yellow, the yellow had given way to the white burst of the morning sunshine and the sun had climbed well up into the sky.

Then they came into a pleasant valley, with steep walls on either hand, and a level floor of cultivated lands checked off with Mexican fences, which are made of stalks of the tornilla bush for uprights, with thorny brush and trailers woven around them and secured with thongs or wire. At close hand such a fence, four feet high and woven thickly enough to bar the eye from a view of the fields, looked impenetrable even to snakes or insects.

"Nothing," said Peter Quince to his companion, "will break through a fence like that?"

"The deer jump it, and some horses," said Juan Garien, "but if they ever catch their legs in the thorns, they never jump again."

So they went on up the valley until they came in view of half a dozen plows at work in a great field, and Peter stopped his horse and rubbed his eyes. Such plows had been used in Bible days, but surely not since! They were simply forks of the encina, cut so that the straight trunk served as the beam of the plow, and the branch, which forked off at an acute angle, was the shear, whose point now drilled the surface of the ground with a perceptible scratch, hardly more. A span of mild-eyed oxen drew each plow, ambling slowly on, seeming to pause and rest with every step. The husband guided the team, the wife followed laboriously, dropping the corn into the little furrow. Peter Quince, as the panting of Bad Luck decreased, and his own ears were attuned to the quality of the silence in that valley, could hear the faint, far voices of the men, all very clear and distinct, but shrunken in volume.

"Who owns that ground?" asked Peter Quince.

"Señor Monterey."

"Ah! We're close to his house then?"

"Not yet. We have been riding on his ground for a long time. Look back!"

He pointed behind them to a rough-headed peak with its side split by the black shadows of a ravine.

"When we passed the crest of that mountain," said Juan, "we rode onto the lands of Monterey. And we may ride straight on until we go past that other mountain before we leave his estate again!"

He pointed forward to a second peak, loftier than its companions and clouded over with the blue of distance, so that it was like a mountain in the sky.

"Why, then," said Peter, amazed, "this man has enough ground to suit a king!"

"Señor," said Juan Garien hastily, "you are right. He *is* a king!"

Peter digested that remark for some time without comment; presently they turned a corner of the valley and came into view of a village. It shocked the eye and the imagination of Peter. It was like a picture he had seen in a book of travels of an African village, save that the buildings were square instead of rounding, but there were the same thatched roofs huddled together. When they came closer, Peter could see that they were built most clumsily, without windows, and with a sack or a blanket serving as a door. Everything, from the molding blades of the dagger plant, which formed the thatch-work, suggested the most repulsive filth, but Peter knew that, though the Mexican may be poor, he keeps his living quarters clean. The wretched condition and the size of the huts appeared much in contrast against the comfortable dimensions of a white-walled house of great size which was seen in the distance, sparkling through the trunks of the trees which shaded it on every side.

"Is this a way for a king to house his subjects?" asked Peter, half in anger and half in curiosity.

"You must ask the señor about that."

Since they had come onto the big estate, Juan had fallen into the habit of referring to his master simply by this title, as though it suggested to him the full dignity of Monterey better than any name of prince or duke.

"Will such a question anger him?" Peter inquired.

"No question angers him," said Juan calmly. "He is above anger."

"The man who lives in that house," said Peter, "can afford to be above anger. He has only to look out at the poor devils in these huts and watch their misery."

"Do you know how the señor would answer that?"

"How then?"

"By telling you the only care he has is to clothe his men in happiness."

"Could he think I would believe that?"

"Listen to me, Señor Quince: Are rich men always happy?"

"Of course not."

"Are very poor men always sad?"

"No again."

"Then you admit that these poor people may be very happy just the same?"

"It is possible, of course."

"It is true, señor. Ask them. You need not even do that. Listen to them singing. Hear their voices. Watch their faces. They are very happy. There are no happier men in Mexico, and they will tell you that they are the happiest people in the world!"

"It can't be true, Juan."

"It is very true, nevertheless. And they will tell you that they owe everything to the señor."

"How do they convince themselves of that?"

"They work for him, to be sure, and in fat years they make a great deal of money for him; but what happens when their crops are small?"

"Well?"

"They would starve. But that is the time that the señor opens his warehouses to them. Each man gets enough. He and his wife and even his smallest child will get enough. Perhaps a poor man gets sick. Are all the children to starve? Is the man to die? No, the señor sends down a doctor to take care of the sick man, and he sends food for the family. That is how he takes care of them. And suppose that a man has a quarrel with one of the overseers, he is not sent away as in other places. He is brought to trial. Who do you think is the judge?"

"The señor?"

"No, no!" laughed Juan triumphantly. "The men of the village are the judges—all the men who wish to come. They are all made to swear to judge truly. Then the overseer speaks and tells how the man was lazy and insolent; then the man speaks and tells how he had too much work put upon him, or how he was sick and so could not do his right work. When they have finished speaking the leader of the men of the village makes a speech. He tells what he thinks on both sides. Then whoever else wants to speak stands up and talks. When they are done, there is a vote. The men of the village say if the overseer or the worker was wrong, and if the worker is wrong how he should be punished."

"They always vote for the worker, I suppose."

"Not at all."

"And if they vote against the overseer?"

"The señor considers what they advise. Sometimes he makes the overseer a worker again."

"Suppose he has a lazy tenant?"

"The men of the village vote on that, also. If the man is lazy they will not want him to get just what they get in bad seasons—the same doctor's care, the same food, you know. They throw out the sluggards."

"Then the men who live on the estate of Monterey get everything except the profits."

"What are the profits, señor?"

"Why, the money, of course."

"But we believe," said Juan simply, "that the money is very little, and that people must live for some better thing."

Peter, abashed, looked down at the pommel of his saddle and said no more. He felt, in fact, that he had stepped a little beyond his depth. This touch of gentleness and nobility disarmed him.

"But here," he said, "we are riding past the house of Monterey!"

"This?" laughed Juan, pointing to the mansion among the trees. "No, no! This is only where an overseer lives!"

"Ah!" said Peter, and rode on. But though he resolutely strove to keep his eyes ahead of him, he could not help glancing to the side. The place was a mansion. What was the wealth of the señor, if his lieutenants were as great as this—the lieutenants whom the vote of the workers seemed strong enough to depose!

It was mid-morning when they passed into a broader section of the valley, where the level floor tumbled into gently rolling hills covered with great evergreens.

"Here is his forest preserve," said Peter, as they neared the wood.

"Here is his park," said Juan, and, as they came into

the heart of the wood, Peter saw that it was no jest; for there were wide stretches of the park which were actually turned into immense gardens with huge lawns, and fountains playing, and riotous colors. And the gardens passed into half wild sections of the woods, and these in turn became wilderness. They rode on for a great distance, though the actual dimensions of the park were no doubt exaggerated largely by the crooked road, which wound here and there.

"Suppose that men are in a hurry to ride to the house of Monterey," asked Peter. "There surely must be a short cut."

"People are never in a hurry who are in the service of the señor," said Juan. "And as for others, they are always glad to take the longer way."

There might have been a double meaning in this remark, and Peter did not care to analyze it.

"How many gardeners," he asked, "work in this park?"

"Hundreds," said Juan. "Besides, when there is nothing to be done in the fields, sometimes he brings in great numbers of workers."

"Does that anger them, to be torn away from their homes and brought to labor like slaves here?"

"Why, it is only a happy party. And every night there is singing and dancing and a real banquet for them."

"And more money?"

"You do not understand even now. The señor pays in happiness, not gold."

Peter shrugged his shoulders. He was beginning to be partly irritated and partly amazed by the characteristics and the powers of this strange man who was a king inside the limits of a republic. But before he had time to retort to Juan's rather contemptuous last remark, he came in sight of a thing which so took his breath that he could not speak.

21. FAIRYLAND

IT WAS A HOUSE, or rather a palace, built loftily against the sky. The treetops shrouded the lower part of it, when he obtained his first glance, and it seemed as high as a mountain. Then he came into a clearing from which he could see the truth.

A winding road swept in a wide curve some hundred and fifty feet up the face of a steep slope, which was almost a cliff, and on the top of the cliff was a huge building of white limestone, which shone dazzling bright in the sunshine. It was not all of one type of architecture. Here it was one story; and here it was four; and here it ran out a long open colonnade; and here there was a square-topped tower, a full hundred feet in height! One could see at a glance that the work of more than one generation had been poured into the place; the fancies, the strength and the dreams of many a man had been turned into stone. And the result was a great hodge-podge, which was yet perfectly beautiful from one end to the other.

There was a great deal of the boy in Peter, and, therefore, his heart leaped and welled almost to bursting at the sight of this corner of fairyland taken from a tale and coined into fact. And he knew, as he looked, that the outside was poor and plain compared with the interior. His exclamation matched his first thought.

"The señor!" cried Peter, for the building seemed to portray the owner.

"It is he," answered Juan, smiling complacently. "Now, you begin to understand some things."

"I begin to understand," said Peter to himself, "that there may be some truth mixed up with a great deal of balderdash!"

When they came out at the foot of the cliff, Peter found himself in a long strip of formal garden which served as a sort of fringe to the forest, and with its delicate flowers and graceful intricacies of design it made an oddly pleasant contrast with the huge and gloomy front of the forest behind it. Among these paths walked a tall man, very old, a little bent, dressed in a suit of light gray flannel, and with a little crimson blossom in the lapel of his coat. His hands were clasped behind him, and the sunshine glinted on the silver beneath the brim of his hat; his attitude was one of solemn and profound thought.

"That is the señor!" said Peter, and his heart went out in instant reverence and kindliness for the man before him.

"That is the gentleman who manages the house of the señor," said Juan Garien.

And Peter bit his lip in his vexation. But the elderly gentleman now saw them and came straight toward them. To Juan he nodded; to Peter he tipped his hat. His attitude was one of a servant, and yet the dignity and the grace of his manner made Peter feel mocked by that air of humility.

"Señor Monterey," he said, "has been eagerly expecting you, Mr. Quince, and I am to learn what can be done to please you in the disposal of Bad Luck."

It was another baffling touch, for how could Monterey have possibly learned of the name of the horse, since that name had not been mentioned to a living soul by Peter Quince since he left the brutal mountaineer who had given the stallion that title? But he determined that he would not be put from his calmness by any such trick information. Señor Monterey might assume the gestures of one who was omniscient, but, though he succeeded among his fellow countrymen, he must learn that in the eyes of Peter he simply made himself ridiculous.

"For my horse," said Peter, "I want only a good feed of hay and grain and clean water. He'll stay anywhere, so long as he gets those things."

The old man clapped his hands, and there appeared, running around the corner of the cliff which was obscured by the outward swing of the roadway, a young fellow apparently as eager for work as a hound is for a trail.

"Take the horse of Señor Quince," said the major-domo.

"He is a hard horse to handle," said Peter.

"It is our business to handle hard horses," said the other with a wave of the hands which dismissed objections.

So Peter, setting his teeth, dismounted and gave the reins to the boy.

"Take the horse to the new box stall, Ricardo," commanded the major-domo.

"And take care of yourself," warned Peter Quince. "He's a tiger!"

Ricardo gave Peter one glance of thanks and then took the stallion with a short rein beneath the bits and held him off to the full length of a stiff arm. He started forward, but Bad Luck flattened his ears and would not budge. A tug at the reins followed and then the gray horse moved with a vengeance. Straight at Ricardo his leap carried him. The boy went down with a stifled cry. The striking front hoof of Bad Luck felled him, and the horse was away like a flash of light, with the bridle-reins tossing.

For the fallen boy the major-domo gave not a glance. His face had turned as white as his hair with rage, and he looked after the stallion, which was racing over the garden beds, tossing the precious mold high above him at every stride. The shout of the steward brought a whole cluster of men into view, and a furious burst of directions followed. They were told in one explosion of words that they were to bring back the stallion uninjured, or they would sweat for their failure for a year to come. They were told that they were to bring him at once, or the penalty would be just as heavy.

Before the words were out of his mouth, half a dozen had leaped into saddles and loosed their horses after the fugitive like a rattling flight of arrows. But what did their eagerness avail them? Never had Peter Quince found a horse that could stand against the gray horse for five minutes of running, and now his empty saddle could be balanced against his weariness. He simply floated away from his pursuers and headed into the forest.

All of this Peter Quince did not see. He had caught up the fallen and motionless figure of Ricardo. The scalp was flayed away from the skull, which showed white, and the blood had gushed over his coat and face until he was a terrible spectacle. To close that wound and bind it hastily with his bandanna was a quick bit of work for Peter. And then Ricardo opened his eyes with a groan.

"Stand up!" said Peter, and dragged him to his feet.

"My head is crushed," gasped poor Ricardo.

"Nonsense!" said Peter. "You can stand, and you can move your arms. No ribs are broken—not a bone broken, and only a knock on the head. You'll be as right as ever in a day or two. You can thank your patron saint, Ricardo, but I'm sorry that Bad Luck used you up."

So saying, covertly he dragged out a handful of coins and poured them into one of Ricardo's coat pockets. And now the frantic words of the steward broke in at last upon the mind of Peter, and he looked away in time to see the gray horse disappear.

"Mr. Quince," said the other, and he turned to Peter a face which was as white with fear as it had been with rage, "I shall return the horse to you at once. And, in the meantime, if you see fit to conceal for the moment from Señor Monterey—"

"I won't say a word to him," said Peter, but all the while he was wondering. What had he been told of the kindness of Monterey? Here was a man who must have been in the service of the family for more than half a generation, and yet he trembled like a boy in fear of a whipping because of a mishap which was only a small part his fault. "And besides," went on Peter, "I'll bring back Bad Luck."

With this he raised a whistle so high and sharp and piercingly shrill that a hawk, which was swooping over the valley on level wings, dodged aside and up and scanned the floor of the valley more anxiously.

"That will bring him," said Peter. "In the meantime, we have only to hope that they don't try to rope him."

"And why?"

"Because he'll run down the man with the rope and the horse he rides on as well. But wait here and he'll come in a moment."

Talking ceased. Then, far off, they heard the crashing of many horses running through the brush of the forest and the shouting of the riders.

"They're coming back on the heels of Bad Luck," said Peter, and, as he spoke, the gray stallion swooped out of the edge of the forest, dashed across the garden, making terrible play with his gouging hoofs as he did so, cast a wild circle around the wondering major-domo and Peter, and then came to a halt, tossing his head with happiness, just before the face of his master. The others now poured out from the trees.

"He had wings, not legs!" breathed the steward. "But how can you handle such a devil of a horse?"

"The señor will probably be able to tell you," said Peter, and, with a smile which Juan Garien was perhaps able to understand, he led the gray horse away, with the steward to guide him.

Fifty feet from the curve of the roadway there was a great arched way which led straight into the heart of the rock. Into this they passed and found themselves in a huge stable. No doubt it had been, in the first place, an immense natural cave, which the action of water had worn away in the limestone, but this cave had been enlarged. Vents had been cut through in the roof rock, so that a free circulation of air could be obtained, and the place had been freely widened on every side, while immense pillars of the living rock were allowed to remain to uphold the surface of the stone. They passed down through a long corridor, from which the side passages suggested spaces, where scores and scores of horses could be kept in comfort; and so they came to a burst of sunshine and the open air beyond. It was a moment before Peter Quince could understand. The Casa Monterey was built upon a hill which was shaped like a wedge, and toward the point of the wedge the stables had been cut through the rock. The major portion of the house itself lay on the rock to the east of the stables. But here was a great box stall, newly hewn from the soft limestone, with a window to let in sun and air and with a wooden flooring for warmth and greater comfort.

Here they left Bad Luck, after he had been unsaddled by the hands of Peter himself, and the major-domo, who now introduced himself as Señor Romiero, led the way toward the Casa Monterey itself.

22. THE JOKER

IT SEEMED to Peter Quince, as he walked up the road to
the house of Monterey, that he was like a common soldier
advancing into the presence of a hostile general. Whether
he would be free, arrested as a spy or thrown into a
common prison he could not tell. Anything was possible.

"Now, Juan," he said, as they approached the door of
the big house, "what am I to find?"

"A surprise," said Juan with his usual grin.

And a surprise was indeed what he found. He was
ushered by the major-domo into a little room in a corner
of the house, a room with a very lofty ceiling, done in
dark wood, with books going up aloft on either hand,
the colors of their rich bindings contrasting with the long
and narrow windows of stained glass which filled two
niches. For the rest, there was a great lamp hung from the
ceiling by an iron chain. Beneath the lamp was a reading
table. Beside the table was a great easy chair. Upon the
table were various luxuries for the smoker—there were
cigars both thin and fat, long and short, dark and pale.
There was everything, and the teeth of Peter yearned to
sink into the butt of a snub-nosed perfecto, whose brown
and oily wrapper told a tale of hidden fragrances. There
were cigarettes, also. They were in a bronze tray, narrow, shallow, and long, with separate compartments for
the separate kinds of tobacco. And there was something
in the intricate carvings which covered the sides of the
tray that made Peter know that those cigarettes had qualities for which a man should be willing to pay with his
soul. Only in the Orient could those twisted and dreamy
figures have been produced by an artist. But, in spite of
all the tobacco which was in sight, there was no smell
of it in the air. Instead, there was a faint odor unlike
anything he had ever come across before. He could not
tell at first whether he liked or disliked it. But he looked
around eagerly for the source of it, and he found that

131

two pale lines of smoke rose from four censers, one on each side of each window.

It was a one-man room, this little library. One might have said that it was conceived by a man who desired to have his favorite books in such a position that he could reach them on either hand without hardly more than rising from his chair; that it was planned by this man and so arranged that it would comfortably hold only one chair, one table, one light. There were two other smaller chairs near the door, to be sure, but they appeared to be half crowded out of the apartment.

But if it were a one-man room, there was a great deal to the man who at present occupied it. Peter had conjured up an imaginary picture of Felipe Monterey as a lean, dark face, heavy black eyebrows, eyes far sunken with weariness and sin, a thin and sardonic mouth, a smile which was a trap for the unwary. He pictured him with slow eyes and restless fingers, a very quiet devil of a man.

What he saw, instead, was a rosy-cheeked fellow of perhaps fifty, bursting with health, his big blue eyes rolling rather prominently under a wide forehead, which sloped back with surprising suddenness. It was a round, jovial face, which made one want to smile instantly. It was the face of one perennially young, though his hair was gray, and his forehead was creeping back and back upon his head. His cheeks swelled with life and happiness. His neck was large with power and reckless vigor. As he leaned forward in his chair, the shoulder muscles threatened to burst the seam of his coat at that point. He now rolled out of his chair and advanced upon Peter with an outstretched hand.

"Peter Quince!" he said. "I counted upon a wait of three days at least. But I see that the dagger in the wall was enough to turn the trick for me!"

And to the utter amazement of Peter he burst into loud laughter, which made him drop the hand which he had been shaking and clasp his ribs. So great was his delight, indeed, that he began to walk up and down the room, alternately striking his hands together and roaring with mirth, then walking again with a thunderous chuckling. One might have said that he had forgotten about the existence of Peter.

"But the rascal actually came so close that he touched the skin!" exclaimed Monterey, turning suddenly upon Peter again.

"He aimed at my head," said Peter. "There was an earnest amount of force behind that throw."

"At your head? Nonsense! He knew that I'd have flayed him alive and rolled him out in the sand for the ants to eat if he'd really harmed you! No, he simply came too close to his mark. Juan!"

His voice rose to a bellow which crammed the little room and flooded far away through the halls with echoes. "Juan Garien!"

A silent step; Juan Garien appeared at the door.

"You touched his skin with that knife," said Felipe Monterey.

"He broke my jaw in return," said Juan, with a lopsided grin.

"You, Juan?" asked Peter, truly amazed. "You threw the knife?"

"Of course. Who else?"

"But I saw it in your belt!"

"That was not the one," said Juan. "With one gone, I have still two more; you see?"

And he produced a long blade. It flashed in his hand and then was restored to his bosom again. Peter Quince sighed. He was beginning to see that he was just a trifle beyond his depth with these men of the Southland. Now a gesture from the señor sent Juan Garien from the room.

"How many like him?" asked Peter. "How many have you as good as Juan Garien?"

"Of that type—none," said the rich man. "That is why I sent him to get you. I picked him from hundreds. He was the best man."

"I suppose that means you sent him on his first visit to me?"

"Of course."

"You knew then that you wanted me?"

"Of course."

"And for what?"

"But that is a long story. Sit down first and smoke."

"Thank you."

He sat down. The tray of cigarettes was offered him. He

lighted one and filled his lungs with aromatic smoke. He blew it forth slowly to taste it the more clearly.

"And still," said Peter, "I am anxious to know just why you have sent for me."

"Because I had heard so much about Peter Quince—because I had heard how he rode through five states and made fools of the sheriffs and their posses—because he got clean away when a hundred thousand dollars or more rested on his head—and all because of a crime which he did not commit!" He lowered his voice. His face lost its enthusiasm and became grave. "But was it not the power of God that helped you, Peter? Was it not that, rather than your skill and cunning?"

"And knowing these things, as you say," said Peter, brushing aside the last question, "why do you want me here?"

"You must have an answer then?"

"I've ridden forty miles for one."

"If you were in doubt you would not have come so far."

"No?"

"I mean that you would not have trusted yourself in my hands."

"You are wrong, Señor Monterey. For I knew that if I came I'd see you face to face."

"And having done that?" asked the señor calmly, with only the ghost of a smile on his lips.

"You say that you know about me," said Peter soberly. "You apparently do not know this: that I am risking everything on the outcome of this interview. If I'm satisfied, all's well. If I'm suspicious, I'll leave this house, walking you in front of me with a gun held at the small of your back!"

"You are confident, my friend," said the señor, and his jaw muscles bulged as he set his teeth.

"I am confident," admitted Peter.

"But would it not be easy for me to deceive you by acting a part and afterward have you at my mercy?"

"I am a gambler by nature, Señor Monterey. If you can deceive me now, you are welcome to whatever advantage you can get over me later. But I warn you now that I'm watching and alert at every instant."

"I know," said Monterey. "And I know that this is

really what brought you up to me—it was the hunger to get at the heart of this adventure. Was it not?"

"It was partly that. It was partly curiosity about you; it was partly curiosity about a girl of whom Martin Avery was telling me not long ago."

He saw Monterey flush under this bluntness, but presently he smiled.

"We are either going to get on very well," said Monterey, "or else we'll fall out entirely."

"Good!" said Peter Quince. "And now tell me why I have been brought here to you."

Señor Monterey left his chair and advanced to the farther end of the room. Then he slid back a panel, and the grim face of El Tigre looked out into the room. It was so real that it seemed to Peter for an instant that the atmosphere around that head was real. Then he saw that it was only a painting. He sank back into his chair with a breath of relief.

"Frightened you, eh?" challenged Monterey.

"Of course!"

The other laughed.

"I am glad you are frank," he said. "But, since you are, I'll try to be equally blunt. I've brought you up here because I want to buy your services, and the service above all that I want is the death of this man, El Tigre. Do you understand?"

"Ah," said Peter Quince, "this is the joker then!"

And folding his hands, he stared deliberately into the face of the portrait. He tried to deny it, but the longer he looked the more convinced he became. No matter that El Tigre had failed to answer his challenge—Peter Quince was horribly, mortally afraid of him—afraid for the first time in his mature life!

23. FACE TO FACE

BUT WHAT Peter asked was simply— "How much?"

"If terms are the only things that hold you back, we'll soon agree. Say what you want. That's the best way to begin." He was smiling in his perfect conviction that Peter was already his.

"I want facts," said Peter.

"Not money?"

"I don't care a whit about that."

Monterey began to stare.

"I want to know just why El Tigre has to die," said Peter.

"Ask the crime records that question," said the rich man.

He lighted a cigar and began to puff at it rapidly until a half-inch coal stood at the end of the tobacco. But the rapidity of his smoking was the only sign he gave of great interest.

"Crime," said Peter, grinning shamelessly, "only wins my sympathy."

"A hundred murders are laid to his credit."

"A score or so are laid to mine," said Peter, "and yet I never drew a gun except in self-defense."

"His crimes are proved by a thousand witnesses," said Monterey.

"So are mine," said Peter. "There are always a thousand liars ready to attack a man who's down! And yet he has followers—even in that town he had followers."

"People fear him, Mr. Quince."

"Perhaps they do, but fear alone won't keep a whole town as quiet as though a snake were charming it. Besides, do you think that everyone down there listens to your wishes because of love alone?"

"That is my boast."

"You are very wrong."

"What man has said that he feared me?"

"I've seen that fear in the eyes of twenty men. You smile, señor, and I see that you are flattered."

"You are very sharp," said Monterey. "However, you err."

"Perhaps."

"But to return to El Tigre. I see what you wish. You are not satisfied with hearing that this man is confessed by everyone to be a plague; you are not content with knowing this, but you want to hear exactly why I consider him an enemy?"

"That's it."

"Will it make it any easier for you to fight if you know that I have grounds for hating him?"

"I tell you, Señor Monterey, that I could not ride a mile after him if I didn't think that there was good ground for hunting him down like a coyote. I've never taken a man trail before, and I don't like the thought of it!"

"I'll give you grounds for hating him then. Let me tell you that I have a niece who has been more than a daughter to me. The story of my hatred for El Tigre is bound up in her."

He composed himself, looking down at the floor with a faint scowl, as though it took a determined effort to force himself even to speak of such a topic.

"My sister was a widow three months after she married," he began again. "She came back to my house, and I took her in due time to Mexico City. There a child was born—this was all eighteen years ago! It was a daughter and she was named Mary, because the American husband of my sister preferred that name during his life. I brought mother and child back to Casa Monterey. My sister was a wretched invalid, however, ever since her daughter was born, and when Mary was five years old, the child was stolen away."

"Kidnapped?" cried Peter Quince.

"That was it. The report was that a horseman had swooped down on little Mary as she was playing in the garden between the foot of the cliff and the woods. The shock of that news killed my sister, Mr. Quince, as though a bullet had been fired through her heart! For my part, being a childless bachelor, there was—"

He paused, his face working a little; then he forced himself to look up again gaily enough.

"Yet it is like facing a gun to think of that day—even to think of it, in spite of the happy times which have come between."

"However, the horseman was—"

"The horseman was El Tigre, of course."

"Why of course?"

"Partially because he was seen and recognized by his size, his horse and his manner of riding; partially because no other man in the country would have had the courage, to speak frankly, to do such a thing to a child living at Casa Monterey. But El Tigre was famous. He is an American, you know, and he had come down into Mexico about five years before."

"But you got Mary back?"

"We followed him hard through the mountains. It was a bright morning when he stole her. It was winter, however, and, as he climbed the mountainside with her, a snowstorm came on. It turned into a perfect blizzard. I can still feel the cold of it burn and sting against my face! I could not breathe, riding into that gale! And in that bitter cold El Tigre had either to abandon Mary, or have her freeze to death in his arms. So he left her behind him. We found her wrapped in his coat, with his slicker around the coat. And—"

"He took the risk of freezing himself for her sake?" asked Peter Quince.

"She meant a fortune to him if he succeeded in carrying her off. Of course, that was why he wrapped her so."

"And left her wrapped in that fashion—left his clothes with her when he abandoned her?"

"I'm not a psychologist."

"Continue, then."

"The man escaped us that day. We took Mary, half frozen, back to Casa Monterey. Then for the first time I knew how much I prized her—partly because she had been so nearly lost and partly because I was so glad to have her back that I had little room to sorrow for the death of my sister. At any rate, there she was, and El Tigre was beaten for once, though it took wind and weather to do it! We thought that was the end of the danger, but a month later the dare-devil made another attempt!"

"What could have made him?"

"Is it hard to guess? He knew then, just as he knows now, that if he got her he could draw on me for half of my fortune for the sake of having her back. He could have gone the length and breadth of Mexico and never collected jewels and gold worth a tenth as much as the price I would pay for Mary. Is that clear?"

"Of course. And yet—"

"Well?"

"I have seen El Tigre. I have even seen his face behind a gun. And he did not look to me like a man who would hunt children for the money he could squeeze out of their parents. I've seen him looking like the tiger you call him, but it was not that sort of cruelty. However—"

"He has made five other efforts in the past dozen years," said Monterey. "In a word, my friend, he has determined that his wits must be stronger than my wits, plus my number of men."

"But you have kept him off."

"I have maintained fifty armed men constantly in and about my house. If I were to touch a bell in this room I could bring ten men inside ten seconds."

"Slow work—slow work, señor," said Peter calmly. "A man could shoot you and run a hundred yards—all inside of ten seconds!" He shook his head. "You should take better care of yourself. Careless guarding, señor."

Monterey smiled. "You are in high fettle today, I observe," he said.

"But," said Peter, "I don't see how I can be necessary to a man who can work miracles."

"You mean by that—"

"You whisk yourself to the town forty miles away and back again in an evening and think nothing of it."

"You refer to the telephone, I see."

"Is it that?" And Peter joined Monterey in the laughter. "I was stupid not to think of that. But does your telephone write out messages at the other end?"

"You mean the one I sent to Juan Garien by the horseman?"

"He really received one then in that way?"

"Exactly. I have one man in the town who acts as my lieutenant. He writes out my messages, and he has learned to forge my signature very exactly. I could not do without his work. It helps me to make the villagers think that I have supernatural agencies at my control. There aren't so many telephones through these mountains, you know."

"I suppose not. How could you lay the wires without letting them know what you were about?"

"I had a big gang of laborers in from the south, working blindly under the directions of one engineer. They buried the wire very rapidly. The line was laid in no time at all in the middle of a stormy season in the winter. Those hunters who happened to see the gang at work simply were too cold to ask questions. The result is that they think I can dash down to the town and back in ten seconds."

"Yet you lift the veil from the mystery for every stranger?"

"For some who care to ask. Have such trifles actually bothered you?"

"I like daylight on everything," said Peter gravely.

"And you see that I have given it to you as well as I could."

"I appreciate that with all my heart."

"And as to the work I have proposed?"

"You have taken care of Mary for eighteen years. Why are you now suddenly afraid?"

"I have always been afraid. I have always been hunting some agency which could remove El Tigre from the scene."

"Frankly, then, what has Martin Avery's seizure by El Tirge got to do with your sudden desire to get me into your service?"

"Can you guess?"

"That Avery has learned something which you are afraid El Tigre will discover by wringing it from him."

"You guess well."

"What is that secret?"

"To continue as frankly as I started, I can't tell you! I wish I could."

"Then, to be just as frank on my side, I cannot enter your service, Señor Monterey."

"Do you mean that? No, wait until this evening. Wait

until you have had dinner with us before you are determined on a course."

"If you wish."

"I do. A man will show you to your room. You are to
be at home here as comfortably as we can contrive it—
that is, until you decide, which need not be for many
days."

With this he touched a bell which was buried in the arm
of his chair. A mozo appeared in answer at the door and
received directions to take Peter to the chamber which
was reserved for him. So Peter saluted his host and went
out. But, as he went up the broad stairway behind the
mozo, he was wondering if it had been mere thought, or
the black beginnings of anger which had brought the
shadow to the forehead of Señor Monterey, as his guest
turned to leave the room. And it occurred to him that if
it had been very easy to enter this house, it might not be
so simple to leave it.

24. FENCING WITH ANOTHER MARY

THE CHAMBER to which Peter was brought proved to be
an entire suite of bedroom, living room, bath, a small
chamber to be occupied by his servant and a little roof
garden, over which the windows of his living room looked,
and onto which he could step through a glass door. And,
to give a crowning touch of luxury to the place, there was
a perfectly appointed little library, whose shelves were
glowing with rich bindings; at one end was a black-
mouthed fireplace, flanked with deep-cushioned chairs, the
very sight of which relaxed the mind. Into one of these
Peter sank and began to think over his situation. Presently
a soft step came up behind him, and he found the mozo
had been replaced by a dapper little individual who addressed him as "monsieur" and wished to know how he
would be dressed for dinner that evening. And when
Peter assured him that he had only the clothes which
were at that moment on his back, the valet with a bow

begged to inform him that he had overlooked a section of his wardrobe and offered to show it to him.

And shown it was. Peter followed him into the bedroom; a closet as large and commodious as a dressing room was opened and found liberally lined with clothes. There were knickerbockers and heavy walking brogues; there were dressing gowns and Tuxedos. In short there were far more clothes than Peter had ever seen appropriated to the use of a single man. For his own part, a pair of overalls, a bandanna, a sombrero, a pair of riding boots and a flannel shirt had been good enough for every day's work, and one "Sunday best" had served for the gala occasions.

He had no choice, however, in selecting what he was to wear that night. The valet guided him with so oiled a deftness that Peter seemed to command instead of being commanded. And in the end he found himself garbed in a Tuxedo and finally looked at himself in amazement— a slender figure in the tall glass, with an air of distinction which Peter had never guessed in himself before. It was like putting on a princely dignity on the spur of the moment.

"But," protested Peter, "how the devil does Señor Monterey keep such a stock of dry-goods on hand? Does he handle all of his guests like this?"

But the valet did not understand. He only knew that Señor Monterey had assured him that he would find the clothes of the new guest in his suite. And there they were! So, in due time, Peter strode down the stairs, rather conscious of the sun-burned face and hands which showed so bronze against the white of his shirt and the white rims of his cuffs. But he was still more conscious of the fact that he was without his revolver.

In those close-fitted clothes he could not possibly have disposed of it in such manner that it would not be visible. He would have needed a little derringer to serve such a purpose as this. But he must not wear a weapon openly in the presence of so gracious a host. It occurred to him more than once, as he was going down, that this matter of outfitting him so carefully with dinner clothes might have been simply a ruse to get his gun away from him and thereby make him helpless.

He set his teeth at the thought, but the suspicion grew lax when he found the señor waiting for him with a smile and a pleasant story and a cocktail in the offing. The cocktail toppled half of Peter's wariness with a crash, and his eyes were opened to a new truth about Monterey. He was no longer a crafty schemer. He was simply a man of whole-souled impulse, who was devoting his life to the happiness of his niece. Monterey spoke of her.

"You are about to find what you started out to discover," said Monterey. "She will be down at once, I hope."

"Are you always reading minds?" said Peter, flushing.

"I have never read a mind in my life," said the señor. "But one may make simple deductions, like the great detectives, you know. And if I find that six women had got you into trouble at one time or another, I may suppose that a seventh will get you out of trouble!" And he laughed so cordially that Peter was forced to join.

"How the deuce," said Peter, "could you have learned so much about me?"

"Don't you realize that you've done enough to get yourself talked about?"

"I suppose so."

"A good many men who hunt for fame would hesitate if they realized that fame is a drag-net which will search all of their past, and that every shady thing they have ever done will be brought up to the surface. We common people drift along largely in darkness. We forget our own sins. But when we step into the public eye, everything is remembered. The search-lights play upon us. Quince, you had hardly started your flight to the south when the search-lights began to play upon you. And when I wished to find out about you, I had only to get in touch with El Paso. They told me even more than I wanted to know. They credited you with a score of murders you could not possibly have committed, and, among other things, they brought to my attention your parentage, the family into which you had been adopted, and six ladies, scattered here and there along your trail, with whom you were said to have had small affairs. You were even accused of being a philanderer."

Peter understood. It was plain enough now that Monterey had only to talk to a police sergeant at the other end of a wire in El Paso in order to hear all of these things.

"They told me also," said Monterey, "that for the past four years you have been credited with sending a steady supply of money back to your foster father. And that, Quince, was what assured me that you were the man I needed. Even in a nation of fighters, you were famous for battle. And yet you were capable of serving a woman. Therefore, I believed that you would be able to crush El Tigre, and that you would be willing to do so. But if—"

His voice trailed away, and when Peter turned he saw her entering the room. He saw no features, but she came to him like the freshness of morning, gracious and young and happy. Whether she were smiling with him or at him, he did not know, and what happened before and during dinner was lost in the golden haze of her beauty. He realized vaguely that Monterey was making a steady stream of conversation; that his own eye was blank and that he must fight desperately to act like a sane man; and then there was an effort to draw him into the talk. There was a question about mining. And he told a tale about prospecting which was so shortened that the point was lost. He saw Mary frown a little in bewilderment, and he told himself that he was acting the part of a consummate fool. But after that he was not bothered again.

The señor took the reins of the conversation entirely into his own hands and managed them gracefully. A good host could make even a statue seem to talk, and this was what Monterey managed with Peter Quince. Then they drifted from the table onto the roof garden which ran down one side of the house. The air was just cool enough to make walking more pleasant than sitting still, so they strolled back and forth until Monterey found that something required him to leave for a few minutes.

"Quince," he said to Mary, "will probably start telling you how beautiful you are as soon as I've gone. He's a famous philanderer. Believe nothing he tells you!" And he retreated, laughing and rubbing his hands. But Mary Porter said not a word for a moment and did not smile at all.

"That's a bad habit of Uncle Felipe's," she said. "He loves to make people seem a little ridiculous."

"But as long as you understand and take no stock in what he says—" began Peter Quince.

"There are so many stories about Peter Quince, though," she said.

"About his philandering?"

"Yes; Uncle Felipe entertained me with half a dozen of them yesterday."

Peter condemned Uncle Felipe behind his teeth.

"Suppose that a man is a prospector," he suggested.

"Are we to suppose, then, that the ladies are gold?"

"Hard rocks, with veins of gold here and there. Men break their hands and their hearts trying to get at the gold."

"That is a sad thing!"

"I cannot see whether or not you're laughing at me."

She turned to him.

"That is much better," said Peter.

"Better?"

"Now the shadow of the moon falls only on one side of your face. It turns you to marble."

"More stone and women!"

"When marble smiles, Miss Porter, then—"

"Let's leave the metaphor. The prospector idea seemed more promising."

"Very well. I was about to say that a prospector, hunting for gold, will tap a thousand rocks with his hammer. And here and there he may break some ground. But he finds the veins pinch out, and the color disappears. But at last he comes to a real vein, and he can tell it at a glance!"

"Well?"

"And that is the way with a man among women. All men are hunting them, you know."

"A prospect to frighten a girl."

"Girls seem to be very brave in the face of such danger."

"Continue then!"

"And I have hunted here and there, it was simply practice, you might say."

"Practice?"

"So that when I found the real gold I should know it."

"I hope," said Mary Porter, "that you'll be fortunate."

"I think that I shall be."

"You are confident then?"

"Of course. I've learned enough to be able to read more in girls than other men do."

"Really?" said Mary Porter, and he could see that she was furiously scornful. But at least she was alive and listening. And, even if it were anger which raised it, there was a flaming color in her cheeks.

"For instance," said Peter, watching her carefully, "even such a clever man as your uncle will make mistakes."

"I have never seen him make one."

"I beg your pardon."

"What is it then?"

"We must step farther away from the door."

"Why?"

"They may overhear."

"Do you think we are watched?" she asked with some contempt.

"I am watched every instant I am in the house," said Peter calmly.

She shook her head, but she obediently moved away from the door which opened into the house. Her lips were slightly parted; he could see that her eyes were brilliant and restless with curiosity. And Peter, watching her, almost forgot what he was about to say.

"And now?"

"I'll tell you how your uncle made his great mistake. He thinks that his most dangerous enemy is camped out yonder, somewhere among the hills. But I have been able to see in a single evening that he is wrong."

"Mr. Quince!"

"But I mean it. He feels that his greatest enemy is El Tigre."

"But the whole world knows that."

"The whole world is very wrong."

"How can that be?"

"His greatest enemy is in this house tonight."

"It is that slippery snake, Don—"

"It is not a man."

"Then I can't understand at all," she admitted. "Who is the great enemy, and why haven't you told him?"

"Why should I tell him? He has brought me here to

kill a man. Why should I tell him that his real enemy is at home—that it is you?"

"I?" cried Mary Porter. "I?"

And she started back from him, as if she feared for his sanity and her own safety.

"You yourself don't know it," said Peter. "That is why I'm rather proud of the discovery."

"I don't wish to offend you, Mr. Quince," she said, "but that is really nonsense! I—an enemy of my dear Uncle Felipe?"

"So great an enemy of his that you are planning to steal away from him the thing which he loves most in all the world."

"Mr. Quince, I suppose that this is all a jest, but it is a very complicated one. You won't seriously accuse me of wanting to rob him?"

"That is the very thing I do accuse you of, however!"

"I am waiting to hear the riddle solved."

"In a single word, what you are planning to steal from him is yourself!"

She only stared at him, while Peter bit his lip. Then she broke into perfectly unaffected laughter.

"This," she said, "is wonderfully exciting and dramatic. I'm almost sorry that there is nothing for me to say, when you have set the stage so well."

25.   PETER MAKES A DECISION

HE WAS in the position of one who has staked his last money upon a hundred-to-one shot. If he had won, his winnings would have been gigantic. But, since he had lost, he was ruined. Yet he only admitted defeat for a single instant. Then he returned to the attack.

"You are sure of that?" he asked her.

"A thousand times sure! Leave my dear Uncle Felipe? I had rather die than even think of it! In the first place, it would break my heart; in the second place, I'm afraid that it would break his."

"I see," said Peter, "that you are blind to your own thoughts. Will you let me try to show you the truth?"

"You are a strange fellow. Of course I'll listen. I suppose every girl likes to talk about herself. But you must hurry. Uncle Felipe will be back in a moment."

"Not at all. He has purposely left us together. I am to stay with you until I have been so charmed that I will be incapable of resisting his proposition."

"Mr. Quince!"

"It is the blunt truth. I am sorry for it! You see that your uncle is human, after all."

"Of course I can't believe you. And, besides——"

"Wait," said Peter, "for I am going to tell you things which you must hear. What I saw first was that you are bored to death with this place."

"With a palace like this?" cried the girl.

"Exactly. It is such a palace that no one comes near you. You have nothing but servants and your uncle near you. What would you give for some girl friends?"

"Ah!" sighed Mary Porter. "But then, everyone has his small unhappiness."

"It is not small. It is so great that it swallows up this whole palace, as you call it. You would give everything for the sake of a ten-minute talk with another girl."

"Of course, that is not true."

"But you would. You'd want to talk it all over—all of this suggestion of mine that you are really tired of the palace, and that you would change it for the sake of a place in a hut, where you could have youth about you."

"I shall not hear you any more," said Mary.

He stepped in front of her, as she turned away.

"If you please!" she commanded sternly.

"Why should you refuse to listen?"

"It is—it is treason to my dear Uncle Felipe to listen to what you say."

"That is not the real reason why you are going. The true cause is that you are afraid of yourself—you are afraid of what effect I may have upon you by continuing to show you the truth!"

"Oh," she cried suddenly, "I hate all your pretended wisdom. I hate it— I hate it! There is not one single ounce of truth in anything you say."

"My dear lady," said Peter Quince, "you protest too much. You make me feel that I have blundered about until I've hit the nail on the head."

"You mean," cried the girl, "that you have been simply bluffing all this time—that you really have been fumbling in the dark?"

"Exactly that."

For some reason this discovery seemed to unnerve her. She slumped back upon a chair and stared up at him.

"What a terrible man you are!" breathed Mary Porter. "I—I'm too exhausted even to think!"

Her wrap had slipped a little from her shoulders. He drew it back over the shimmering white. Still she did not stir, but lay helplessly in the chair, watching him. She was like one in a sick bed, unnerved by shock.

"Why have you done this?" she asked faintly at last.

"Put yourself in the place of me. Suppose that you met a man who told you of an immense treasure he had seen, but from which he had been frightened away. Suppose that you heard such a description of the treasure that you were on fire to see it and touch it. The man tells you that it is a dangerous thing to attempt, and that if you once see the treasure you will never die happy until you possess it—what would you do?"

"I should die trying to find it!"

"You are right, of course. That is what I determined. Well, you are the treasure, and Martin Avery was the man who talked to me about you!"

"Poor Martin Avery!" she said.

It meant a great deal to Peter—this remark. It meant that she did not care to take offense at the declaration which he had just made, and, instead, she was willing to turn the talk upon a side topic. It meant, moreover, that Avery had made no impression upon her.

"What did Avery discover that El Tigre wanted so much to know and that your uncle feared so much he might find out?" asked Peter.

She shook her head.

"I haven't the slightest idea what you mean."

"Let it go then. To come back to what we have been talking about."

"But I don't want to come back to it!"

"Are you so afraid of the truth?"

"It is not the truth, but—"

"Why," said Peter, "I saw the shadow in your face as I met you. The only guessing I did was about the cause of the shadow, and you see that I hit it right the very first chance I took. If I leave you, what are you going to do about it?"

"About what, Peter Quince?"

"About your lost life here."

"Do you call this a lost life?"

"Don't you? Haven't you spent hundreds of hours dreaming of the other things? Haven't you seen yourself surrounded with a bevy of pretty girls and the worship of young men?"

"No, no!"

"You're not telling the truth. Of course you have. Every time you look in your mirror you see something which tells you that you ought to be where other young people are."

"I'm going in," said Mary Porter, and stood up.

"Wait! I'm not through."

"I won't listen."

"You must. I say that every day of your life you have been seeing yourself living and laughing among your peers. And wherever you have gone in your dreams you have been happier than you are in Casa Monterey. Isn't that true?"

"Let me go past you, Mr. Quince!"

"Not a step till you hear the rest. I say that if your dreams are happier than this place, there are still greater happinesses than the dreams. They are nothing. You have been thinking of gold. But I can pour your hands full of it."

"You?"

"By setting you free!"

"Don't say it!"

"It's cowardly to turn your back on temptation. Face it out."

"Let me past—I beg you to let me go in!"

"Not a step!"

He caught her hands and held her. There was not much effort needed. For she was trembling so that a child could have stopped her, and he controlled her with a raised hand.

"You are dying in this place," cried Peter softly. "You are throwing away the sweetness and the blossom of your life here. It is worse than death. Let me tell you the naked truth. If you were away from here—where men could see you—every day you would make a hundred men stand straighter and swear that they had seen a glimpse of heaven!"

"Oh, if you talk to me so, what shall I do?"

"Open your ears and your heart and hear the whole truth."

"I shall never be happy again for an instant if I keep listening to you!"

"Then you admit—"

"Nothing!"

"I can feel the beating of the pulse in your wrist. It is wild and hurried. And it keeps singing to me that you believe me—that I have told you the truth—that I have broken down the wall of self-deceit—that you know you have been in prison, and that I am showing you the open blue sky outside."

"Oh," she sighed suddenly, "God help me—and God help poor Uncle Felipe!"

He released her hands, and she sank back into the chair, with her forehead bowed into her palm. And Peter felt as though he had brutally struck her down. She had been wonderful—past words in her pride and her haughtiness—but now that she was beaten it seemed to him that his heart would break for the worship of her. He dropped to his knees, and the perfume which was entangled in her hair floated dimly about him.

"Mary," he said, "if I have hurt you, it is only because I want to make you happier than you have ever been before. I don't aspire to you. All I want is a chance to serve you—to take you from these walls and let you go where there is a whole garden—where the world can see that you are the sweetest and the purest rose among them all."

"Hush," she said, "I have been trying to hate you, and now you will make me forgive you, Peter Quince."

So he waited without saying a word, watching her

bowed head, wondering over her, loving her with a sad seriousness.

At last she said: "Only one thing, Peter."

"I am listening," he answered, feeling that his name had been sanctified.

"You must promise not to blame Uncle Felipe. He has only been keeping me safe from that terrible creature—El Tigre!"

"That is why," said Peter, "that El Tigre must die. I did not see before, but now I know that El Tigre has to die—simply in order that you may go away with me. You will promise that, Mary?"

"Hush!" she whispered again, and he saw that she had already heard too much.

So he rose beside her, lifted her up, and they began to walk up and down through the moonlight on the roof. Then she stopped suddenly. He felt her hand press hard upon his arm.

"But suppose that Uncle Felipe should have seen us talking together?"

"Well?"

"That is too terrible to even think of!"

"We will not think of it, then."

And Uncle Felipe came out at that instant upon the roof, whistling. The careless tune was like a mockery of a tragedy which had just taken place there. He joined them, talking of something—nothing.

"And in ten minutes," he said, "I suppose that you have managed to find out a great deal about one another?"

If Felipe Monterey had been the most ignorant of fools, he could not have helped suspecting something. He jerked his head toward Peter Quince, and Peter was glad indeed that the moon had just slipped behind a cloud.

26. A BRAVE COWARD

EL TIGRE abandoned his Spanish and relapsed into the type of English which is spoken by some thousands between the Rockies and the Sierra Nevadas.

"Now, Avery," he said, "we're going to have our last business talk together. You understand?"

Martin Avery could not control his trembling lips for a moment, but then he managed to answer that he was ready to be questioned, and all the while he eyed his captor with a fascinated interest. For the bandit had dragged him before a sort of high bench which served for a table in the hut, and his huge long legs sprawled under it, while upon its top stood the whisky bottle and the cup into which he poured the refreshment. He splashed a liberal portion into it now and pushed it across the board to his captive.

"Drink hearty, Avery," he commanded. "You'll be needing it soon, maybe—which I ain't taking on myself to do no prophesying. But you better get together all the strength you can."

Martin Avery shook his head. "I don't use the stuff," he declared.

"Teetotaler, eh?" grinned the outlaw.

"I am."

"Well," said the outlaw, "I got no use for you nor for none of your kind. But let that slide. What I want now is information. I ain't going to bother you for none of them little details that some folks might put a lot of store by. All I want is the big things."

"Such as what?" asked Martin Avery.

"Such as what you seen in the underground part of Casa Monterey."

Martin Avery shrank and then shook his head.

"I saw nothing—I don't know what you mean, Mr.— El Tigre."

"You was seen to go inside," he said. "You was seen

153

to go in, and I know well just where you went in. All you got to tell is what you seen inside."

"Nothing," said the poor fellow. "I've seen nothing."

"What d'you mean by that?" thundered El Tigre. "Are you calling me a fool?" And, as rage and black blood swelled his throat, his beard bristled like the mane of a wolf.

"I'm calling you nothing," sighed Martin Avery, almost speechless with dread. "I mean—I have given a solemn promise that I would not state what I had seen."

"A promise, eh? Well, son, I'm going to teach you to forget that promise. Understand? I'm going to make you forget it."

"I hope not," said Avery, trembling violently. "My honor would be lost if I forgot."

"Honor!" said the bandit. "I'll say what's honorable and what ain't around this here camp. I've stood for a pile of chatter and back-talk from you, Avery, and that's got to be stopped!"

He beat his fist upon the table as he spoke, and the latter was crushed halfway to the floor by the weight of the blow. The whisky bottle skidded off, rolled across the floor, and crashed to splinters against a stone. El Tigre had made a vague effort to reach the falling bottle, and when he saw that the attempt was futile, he had laid his hand upon his gun, as if that aid in all times of trouble must be of assistance to him even then.

"It's the last," he said finally. "There ain't another drop in the whole bloomin' camp. There ain't another taste of redeye closer'n fifty miles away. There ain't nothing but that murderin' mescal and such rot to drink."

Here he turned furiously upon Martin Avery.

"And you're the cause of it!" he roared.

"I'm terribly sorry!" gasped Martin. "Upon my word—"

"You lie!" cried the other. "You're glad to see the booze gone—you're proud to see it spoiled. Now, listen to me, Avery, you skinny rat. I'm going to have the truth out of you, or else bust you to smithereens. Avery, tell me what you seen under Casa Monterey, and tell me pronto!"

Avery had shrunk away from this thundering torrent of words until his shoulders were pressed against the wall. Then, when he could retreat no farther, his wretched glance sought the door. But flight was worse than useless. Even if the revolver in the expert hand of the outlaw did not pour a stream of lead into him before he had left the hut, there were a dozen others outside ready to turn him into a sieve at a word of command. They would even rejoice in the practice at a moving target.

"You hear me?" yelled El Tigre.

"I hear you," moaned Avery.

"Will you talk?"

"I've given my word of honor."

"Your word of fury and hell fire! Will you talk?"

"I dare not!"

"I'll help teach you to dare!"

He bellowed a word in Spanish, and two stalwart rascals sprang into the shack. "Your guns!" roared the bandit.

Their revolvers came out with the oily ease of long practice. They were held ready and pointed upon Martin Avery.

"Now, you fool," cried the leader, "do you talk, or do you feed the buzzards?"

Martin Avery fell upon his knees and with his hands shut out the impending doom.

"God help me—God forgive me for my sins!" cried Martin.

"Will you talk?"

"Give me time."

"Not a minute! Will you speak, or do you get two slugs of lead through your fool head?"

"Merciful heavens!"

"There ain't no mercy here. There's nothing but facts."

"God receive me and forgive me!" sobbed Martin Avery, and shrank into a limp huddle against the wall.

The two bandits leveled their guns. Their teeth glinted at the master as they waited for the final signal. But El Tigre had risen stiff and tall with amazement behind the table and was staring down at his victim. Rage and wonder were equally in his face, and a brief gesture made his men put up their guns.

"What is he?" asked one of the men.

"He is a wise fool and a brave coward," said El Tigre in swift Spanish. "Up with him!"

They jerked Martin Avery to his feet, and he hung helpless on their arms. All the color had left his face, and there was the look of death already in it.

"One more chance, Avery! Will you take it? One more chance for you to go scotfree—not a harm done to you —sent safe and sound to the other side of the river. What do you say? Will you talk?"

The wretched Martin Avery closed his eyes with a groan.

"I've given my word. Get it over with—this is killing me ten times instead of once!"

"Kill him deader than a stone then!" roared the outlaw, and the two guns leaped obediently, eagerly from their scabbards, hung in the air, and then fell harmlessly back at the sharp command of the chief.

"Leave him to me," said El Tigre. "Go out and leave him to me!"

They obeyed regretfully, throwing villainous glances back at one who had so nearly been their victim.

"Now," said El Tigre, when they were alone again, "I've shown you that I have men who'll do my work. I've only to give them a signal—no more'n the lifting of one eye—and you're done for. Understand?"

Avery nodded convulsively. He lay back in the chair into which he had fallen, his whole body twitching now and again, as the recollection of the terrible peril came again through his mind.

"I understand," he breathed.

"And when you're dead, it's a mighty easy thing to get rid of the body."

"Yes!" gasped Avery.

"Then talk sense and tell me what I want to know."

"My honor—"

"Honor? Say, man, ain't we all seen you show yaller?"

"My sacred promise—"

A look of wonder again passed over the face of the outlaw, and there was respect mingled with his amazement.

"You'd die for the sake of making that word of yours good?" he asked.

"I'll have to die for it," groaned Avery.

"Because of Monterey?" went on the other with sudden heat again. "But I tell you, Monterey is worse than I am. He's a thousand times worse than I am! I could tell you what he's done, and the tale would—" He paused and began to stride up and down the shack, glowering at Martin Avery with a sort of honest indignation, as though he had caught the latter in the midst of a mean action.

"Well," he said at last, "I'm a fool—I'm ten times a fool. But I can't put this bluff through. If I was to give you a taste of a quirt on your bare back, I figure that you'd weaken fast enough. But somehow I can't quite do it. I'm going to let you through with this, Avery."

"God bless you!" moaned the wretched man.

"Bah!" snarled the other and, striding past his captive, he advanced through the door into the outer sunshine. There he was greeted with a volley of questions in the eyes of his companions, but he waved them away.

"What is the news of the gray horse?" he asked.

There was no answer other than a deep murmur of discontent.

"Who has seen him last? Who has been watching?" continued El Tigre. "Guillermo, it was you?"

The lieutenant rose, stretched himself, yawned and made answer.

"Perhaps it was I," he murmured.

The retort of El Tigre was as swift as the leap of his namesake. He crossed the distance between himself and Guillermo in the twinkling of an eye. For all his great bulk, his speed was the speed of a leaping cat. Guillermo was taken by surprise. No doubt he had seen his chief in action twenty times, but he had never seen his attack without more provocation than this.

He reached for his gun to meet that charge, but in his excitement the front sight caught against the polished leather which lined the holster on the inside, and his draw was delayed an instant, just such an instant as a fist is delayed as it ends a short feint and then jabs out again to complete a punch. It was enough, however, to ruin the chances of Guillermo in the fight. The gun was only half out of the leather when the hand of El Tigre reached him. Even then the leader did not strike. He merely caught the gun arm of his lieutenant above the wrist, and the mere compression of his hand was enough to make the other drop the revolver from nerveless fingertips. At the same time the twist of El Tigre brought Guillermo into his arms.

"You are finished?" asked El Tigre through his teeth.

"You are lucky," answered Guillermo, equally soft of speech and repaying his chief, glare for glare. "You are lucky. Except for that—"

"I should be a dead one, Guillermo?"

"You should, and you are nearly a dead one now."

"Eh?"

"Look at the men."

A side glance at the others made El Tigre aware that there was mutiny in the air.

"What's in the air?" he asked.

"Come aside with me and I'll tell you."

27.　EL TIGRE RIDES ALONE

NEVER WAS a treaty of peace more swiftly concluded. The few muttered words, the quick glances—these had been all. Then they walked away together among the rocks, leaving behind them the band, every man of whom was quivering with excitement. When they were alone El Tigre began:

"We've been together a long time, Guillermo. Why has this had to come between us?"

Guillermo had sought comfort for his shaken nerves, as usual, in the manufacture of a cigarette. He lighted it, broke it in his fingers and made another. All of his anger and nervousness showed in those active fingers, thin as the claws of a bird.

"Why are the others," countered Guillermo, "watching you like eagles?"

"Are they doing that?"

"They are doing that."

A little silence came between them.

"Very well," said El Tigre. "If they are tired of me—they may all go. That is all. I worked freely without them. I can do as well again."

Guillermo smiled.

"That may do for them. You and I know that that is not true, El Tigre."

"What?"

"We know that is not true." His rapid Spanish almost baffled the attentive ear of the chief. "If you get rid of these men, one of them will sell you to the law."

"That has been tried."

"By fools who thought they knew everything, but who really knew nothing. These men up here, however, know all of your places. They could sell the location of every hiding place you have. What would you do then?"

"Cut their traitor throats!"

"That is easy to say."

"Guillermo, do you think it means this?"

The lieutenant nodded.

"You yourself?" asked the chief.

"After today I can never ride behind you again."

"Why, Guillermo?"

"You made me seem like a child before the others. I shall have to kill a man before they respect me again."

"And that man may be me?"

"If I am lucky," said Guillermo frankly, and his black eyes glittered at El Tigre, "you must be the man."

The chief shrugged his great shoulders.

"Be a wise man and keep away from me," he said. "I have beaten you once, and if you come at me again, I'll wring the head off your shoulders. Now, go on and tell me why you and the rest are showing your teeth at me."

"Where were we camping three days ago?"

"You know as well as I. A very pleasant little valley with everything that a man's heart could desire."

"And where did we camp the next day?"

"We were riding," said El Tigre, frowning at the questions like one unused to answering.

"And where were we camped last night?"

"We were riding again last night."

"And why have we been racing through the mountains as though a thousand men were hunting us?"

"Because—is that why the teeth are shown, Guillermo?"

"Is it a bad reason?" asked that slender and handsome warrior. "Are we children to run away before one grown man? He had killed one of our best. Ranjel Verial is dead. And yet we run away from his killer. Must our own deaths go unrevenged in the same way? And why are we running from a man who wants nothing, he says, but to meet El Tigre face to face. It is the first man who has ever dared to ask for that. And this is the first time El Tigre has turned away and tucked his tail between his legs and run like a frightened cat!"

The big hand of El Tigre rose like a club, then dropped, and the strong fingers were twined around the butt of the gun.

"This is the whole story?" he asked.

"In the name of the seven saints," groaned Guillermo, "is it not enough? What will be our reputation among other men when it is known that we follow a man who runs away and will not face such a boy as this Don Pedro?"

The chief shrugged his shoulders.

"It is the end of the band then?" he asked.

"It is the end of the band. And if it is the end of the band, it is the end of El Tigre."

"All of that is true."

"Then be yourself once more, El Tigre! Kill this coyote who dares to run on your trail."

"Guillermo, if you knew who he was you would never ask me to do this thing."

"Kill him, or be sold by your men. Why, they'll murder you in your sleep and sell you the next day. They feared you yesterday; they loved you the day before; but today they despise you!"

And so the truth came solidly home to El Tigre. Either Peter Quince must die, or he himself must be destroyed. It was a grim decision to make, but being a grim man he made it in the way his lieutenant had expected.

"After all," muttered El Tigre, "no one but myself dreams of the truth. Why not?"

He glowered at Guillermo.

"Go tell the others that Señor Quince has ridden his last day on the trail of El Tigre."

"Take your own messages," said Guillermo, sneering. "I have served you the last day."

In another instant a great hand had throttled him and dragged him to his knees.

"Now go!" commanded El Tigre, and he flung Guillermo away.

And Guillermo? He would have died a thousand times rather than suffer such an indignity from the hands of any common man or men, but to him, even as to all the others, there was something more than common mortal in El Tigre. He fumbled at his throat, gasped back his breath, and staggered away to execute the command. El Tigre went straight back to the shack.

There he found Martin Avery seated with arms sprawled out over the table and his face hidden in his arms. He tapped him on the shoulder, and the young engineer sprang to his feet.

"Avery," said the bandit, "you're a free man now. I'm going on bigger business than the business in which I was trying to use you. Get out of the camp and get out of the country. If you come in my sight again I may do you a harm for the sake of the trouble you have made for me." As Martin Avery gaped at him he continued: "The horse for you is hobbled outside the door. Go get him."

"But when your men see me go—"

"They'll know I told you to. They'll know that you're not trying to escape from them!" And he smiled with a commingled mirth and scorn.

So Martin Avery went out with trembling hands and unloosened the horse and saddled and bridled it. But the dark-skinned ruffians gave him not a glance. He seemed to be no more to them than the rocks which littered the side of the mountain. When he was finished, El Tigre himself threw a roll of blankets behind the saddle and strapped them in place. Then he hung a leather bag of provisions beside the knee of the rider. In the holster he dropped a long revolver.

"For the looks of the thing," grinned El Tigre. "Because I sure hate to see a growed-up man riding without a gun in sight. Looks worse'n if he'd rode off and forgot his hat!"

"El Tigre," said Martin Avery, "I—I don't know what to say to you!"

"Don't say nothing to El Tigre," said the outlaw. "But you're a white man, Avery. I s'pose that you figure yourself out to be a coward. But lemme tell you that I figure you to be a hero and a mighty big one. Understand? I don't want you to talk to El Tigre, but I want you to shake hands with a man that was once as white as you are. Shake with John Quincy, Avery! Ever hear that name?" And his grin broadened as the other shrank and then stared with a redoubled interest. The slender hand was lost in the huge paw.

"So long, Avery."

"El—I mean, Quincy—I wish that I could take you back with me and—"

"And collect the reward? Sure you do, and a lot of better men than you wish the same thing!"

"No, what I meant was—"

"You're talking too long. Run away, Martin Avery."

And Martin Avery obediently rode off down the hill. When he was gone the chief picked his own saddle off the hook from which it was hanging and went out to the group of saddled horses. There he picked out the giant chestnut and saddled and bridled him. After that he rode down the slope, and as he went he noted that not an eye was turned after him from the gang. They continued their smoking and their card playing, with a saddle blanket as a table. They continued as though nothing except themselves lived within a thousand miles of them. But El Tigre could read the very expression of their backs, and he knew that one and all were thinking of him and the fact that he was riding down to wipe from their trail the man who had killed Ranjel Verial. They were thinking of that, and they were thinking, every one of them, that it was a task worthy of any two ordinary men. When he came back from that task there would be no doubt about their obedience.

And yet, when El Tigre thought of that combat, he sickened. If only he could speak three words to the youth, all would be well; but there would be no time for that. The instant they glimpsed one another the bullets were certain to start flying.

28. A TRUCE

Now FOR four hot, laborious days Peter Quince had been pushing in on the trail of El Tigre. Wherever he crossed other men, he told them frankly what he was doing, and he asked them to point out the way to him. The reply which he received in the villages was invariably laughter, and yet they would also point out to him, still laughing, the direction in which El Tigre was supposed to have marched. And, as a matter of fact, he soon saw that the reason they told him so much was because they thought the whole affair must be a hoax, and that he was simply a recruit trying to join the famous leader.

The third day had carried him into higher and rougher mountains. He was living on the fish he caught in the streams and striking doggedly on at the steady pace which Bad Luck was able to maintain indefinitely—which he had kept up during the long flight from the States. On the fourth day he lost the trail, worked half the morning to recover it and, when he had found it, made his brief noon camp, then went briskly ahead up the side of the mountain.

It was a black mountain, such as he had never seen before. There were towering pinnacles of glistening black which looked like blown glass, and there were stretches of the broken rock of a more sooty appearance, and the busy hoofs of Bad Luck raised little clouds like smoke, which the wind floated away. Even the trees and the shrubs along the slope seemed black from the sooty dust which had settled upon them and clung. As for Bad Luck, he was rapidly turning from a light gray to a dull, drab gray. And then, crossing a shoulder of the mountainside, Peter heard a great voice behind him calling: "Peter! Peter Quince!"

He looked back and knew that he was lost. There upon the immense chestnut horse he had seen before was the towering form of El Tigre. It made him upon the more

163

slender stallion seem a mere child upon a colt. And all at once he felt a wave of impotence pass over him, just as it had struck across him when he first faced the big man in the patio of the tavern. He had met his match, and he knew it. Perhaps more than his match, and certainly he had less than no hope in this battle.

He pulled at his gun, though the weapon of El Tigre was already balanced in his hand. But it was a hopeless effort, for it stuck in the holster. He jerked it forth and seemed to hear the voice of the big man dinning at his ear: "For God's sake don't shoot!"

That, however, must have been a dream. Perhaps the weapon of the outlaw had missed fire, but his own would not! It flashed up to the mark, he touched the trigger, and El Tigre leaned forward from the saddle and fell upon the ground.

The chestnut wheeled with a neigh like the cry of an angry eagle and fled down the slopes, but Peter did not watch the magnificent fellow go. All his mind and his heart were lost in the contemplation of the giant who lay stretched upon the ground. Even had he seen the lightning strike, he would have doubted the fall of the monster. But he stole closer, urging Bad Luck step by step. There was no stir or tremor in the fallen mass. Then the wind lifted the wide sombrero from the fallen head and rolled it away. It set the long hair of the fallen man floating, and for the first time it seemed possible to Peter Quince that the giant was actually dead.

He threw himself from the horse and ran to examine the wounds. Only with an effort could he turn that great bulk of inert flesh and bone. Then he saw that crimson was pumping from a hole in the breast of El Tigre. In his fall he had struck his forehead against a small rock edge, and that was the reason his eyes were still closed in insensibility—unless the bullet had actually touched the heart.

But Peter found the pulse quivering, and now he hesitated. No doubt that this wound was mortal, and doubtless it would be best to let the man die at once, painlessly, without letting him recover only to look up into the face of the conqueror.

This thought, however, he dismissed at once with a shudder, and he began to work over the wound, stanching the flow of blood as well as he could. And to his astonishment he found that it was not so hard to do. Presently the bleeding had ended, and he had discovered, as he stripped the shirt from El Tigre to make the bandage, that the skin of the outlaw was as white as his own. El Tigre was Mexican in name only.

This made him work all the harder, and when he had completed the bandage he dragged the big wounded man into the shadow of a tree and gave him a stiff dram of brandy out of his saddle flask. It had an instant effect upon the outlaw. He opened his eyes, looked wildly about him, and then fastened his glance upon Peter. And he smiled! Yes, it seemed to Peter that there was actually joy and recognition in the smile of the chief.

He used the canteen to pour a long drink of water down the throat of the wounded man and then tried the brandy flask again. And this time the bandit looked up with a clear intelligence shining under the frown on his brows.

"Peter!" he said faintly.

"Well?" said Peter, and wondered why his heart had leaped at the sound of that voice.

"Is it the end?"

"I don't know," said Peter Quince. "I hope you'll pull through."

"I do—for my sake—and for yours!"

He closed his eyes again and left Peter to ponder over this strange remark. What it could mean to Peter if the man died was worthy of wonder.

El Tigre did not speak again for fifteen minutes, but during that time Peter found the pulse of the stricken outlaw was growing more and more steady. The color began to return to his face. He was still in a serious condition, but it was perfectly plain that this was not a mortal wound. And immediately the position of Peter became painfully complicated. He could not take in his prisoner in this condition, and if he stayed with him, El Tigre's band would recapture their leader together with his conqueror.

There was a temporary retreat, at least, near by. Two immense boulders jutted forth like arms from the side of the mountain, and the space enclosed was well secured.

There was only a yard-wide entrance. For water there was a spring not fifty feet away. For food there were the contents of his saddlebags as well as what his rifle could bring in. But the greatest danger was simply that the other outlaws would sweep down to the rescue of their leader and overwhelm him. He could only hope that he might be able to hold them off until their patience was tired. Besides, what wolf pack will endanger itself for the sake of a stricken leader?

With this in mind he prepared at once for a siege. The major preparations were cut comparatively short, for, as he issued from the door of his covert, a deer wheeled in the open space and dashed for cover. Peter Quince dropped the fine fellow and cleaned him on the spot. When he had dragged the carcass in, he and his prisoner were secure of provisions for some days. Firewood was the next necessity. But this was hardly more difficult to procure than had been the meat. He found a dead and fallen trunk not far off. A few minutes' work with his hand ax severed it into sections which he dragged into the shelter. Next he filled the canteen with water and finally converted his slicker into a great water sack which he filled and then carried in.

That last trip, however, was not made any too soon, for something whistled in the air and clicked against the stone as he entered the refuge, and immediately afterward the loud and metallic ring of a rifle report beat against his ears, while presently distant echoes rolled in, plumbing the thin immensities of the mountain spaces. The band of El Tigre had come upon the trail of the wounded leader at last, and there would be plenty of action for Peter from now on!

Hastily he made the last preparations. He had water, food and fuel. If there were a storm, he could build shelter enough under the rocks. As for his defenses, there were only a few holes of any size in the stone walls, and these he now blocked with heavy rocks. If they chose to attack his case would be hard indeed, but he felt reasonably assured that they would not attempt to rush him by day and take their chances with the gun which had brought down their formidable chief. They would confine their attacks to the dark of the night. So Peter could sleep in

the day and waken at night. Yet if he slept in the day, he
must bind his prisoner.

On the whole, it was an ugly predicament, but Peter
was already beginning to hope. Half a dozen more bullets
spattered against the rocks of his fortification. Voices
shouted in the distance, and then there was silence. So
Peter turned to his prisoner and found that his eyes were
wide open, clear, unstained with the shadows of fever.

There was a decided improvement.

"And so," said El Tigre, "you are in a bad place,
señor?"

"Talk English," said Peter Quince. "Why is my position
so bad? I have only to wait until night and then make a
break down the hill."

"And leave me behind, however!"

"I could use the butt of a gun on your head, El Tigre,
and when I get back my reward will be just as great as
if I had you with me. I can take enough proofs of your
death."

"That sounds like strong talk," said the outlaw without
the slightest emotion. "But I guess you'd weaken before
you done that."

"You'd count on that?"

"Nacherally. You're one of them fools that carries a
chicken heart around with you, and that makes a pile of
difference between killing a man standing and lying down."

"Don't you?" asked Peter, watching the other with a
sneer of disgust.

"Why should I? You'd kill him just as dead one way as
the other. But I know your kind. You'd stick on that way
of doing things. It ain't what you do—it's the way you do
it."

"You've talked enough," said Peter, gritting his teeth.
"You're working up danger for yourself."

"You think so? I tell you that I know your kind. You're
trapped here. That's all!"

"They'll never put hands on me," said Peter. "I know
these Mexicans."

"How d'you know 'em?"

"I've read about 'em, and I've heard about 'em."

"You've heard a package of lies," said the bandit,
"from a lot of skunks that got run out of the country. And

you've read a lot of rot by fools that take a ride across country on a train and don't see nothing except what the train windows are frames for. They do the talking. Them that knows are too busy living to bother with words. But you think that these boys of mine out yonder won't try to get me out?"

"Why should they throw away half a dozen lives to get you?"

"You talk like an American," said El Tigre. "If they was Americans—my own countrymen—I'd figure that a lot of crooks and long riders might play that sort of a game. But these here are Mexicans. Listen to me. An hour ago them boys were getting pretty sore at me because I was running away from you. They were ready to fight me because I was making them lose all their dignity. A Mexican loves his dignity like a dog loves its skin. But now that I'm in trouble, they'll wait out yonder till they starve, but they'll sure get me out! That's the way. Every one of them is remembering right now all of the good things that I've done for 'em. They don't forget. It's easier for 'em to die than it is for 'em to forget."

Peter Quince heard these words with grim discontent, for he recognized the truth which was in them as clearly as if it shone. And, as if to put greater emphasis on what had just been said, his attention was called outside by a loud crunching and rumbling sound over the rocks, and he looked out to see a huge trunk being rolled toward the door of his shelter by invisible hands.

There might be a dozen men lying prone behind that log and working it toward him. They were so perfectly sheltered from bullets that they could bring it straight up to the door of the shelter and then rush. One of them would go down before his bullets, but the others would be too close to be injured. He could not fire effectively more than once before they would be upon him. Would they risk the rush? There was no doubt of that in his mind from the busy fashion in which they rolled the log toward the covert.

His exclamation called a question from the outlaw. He wanted to know what was happening, and Peter told him gloomily.

"Call to them," said the wounded man, "and get their attention."

"Why should I do that?"

"Do what I tell you, boy," commanded El Tigre.

And Peter could no more have denied that voice than if he had been a child. He shouted. The rolling of the trunk ceased for an instant, and in the interval El Tigre called: "Guillermo!"

There was an answering call from behind the log.

"Come to me. Señor Quince will respect the truce. Come at once and let the log remain where it is."

Without an instant's hesitation Guillermo rose from the place behind the log and stepped slowly forward. He paused at the entrance to the covert and surveyed the two inside. Then he walked on toward El Tigre. The latter beckoned, and Guillermo dropped upon his knee. For an instant the fallen leader murmured at the ear of his lieutenant, and then Guillermo sprang to his feet and turned upon Peter Quince a face dark with scorn and horror.

"That?" cried Guillermo. "Is that the man?"

"He knows nothing of it," said El Tigre.

"Bah!" sneered Guillermo. "But we will give him ten minutes to be gone. If he is still here after that, we finish him."

And his gesture completed the sentence. He turned on his heel and walked back to the log and dropped behind it.

29. A HAPPY MAN

"YOU SEE," said El Tigre, "that there is now a gate open for you. If you climb into the saddle and ride away during the next ten minutes, you will be allowed to go safely."

Peter sat down on a stone and looked the outlaw in the face. "Why did you do it?" he asked.

"Because," said El Tigre, "when I am walking around again and able to sit the saddle, I want to hunt you for myself. Wouldn't amount to much if you were wiped out by a dozen men in a rush."

"Very well," said Peter Quince. "You are saving me for a killing when you are able to do it yourself. And, as a matter of fact, I begin to think that you could do it whenever you chose!"

"Me?" exclaimed the big man, and blinked at Peter in the utterness of his astonishment at this admission.

"You held your fire," said Peter, "when you could have filled me full of lead. You were behind me. You could have killed me six times while I was turning and getting out my gun. Why didn't you do it?"

"Gun missed fire," said El Tigre, and looked calmly straight into the face of Peter Quince.

"Was it a gun missing fire that sent Guillermo out of this place and that made him look at me as though I were a leper?"

"Guillermo has queer ways of his own."

"I tell you, El Tigre, that the same thing that kept you from shooting at me was the same thing that sent Guillermo out of the place!"

It was rank guessing, but he saw that the shot struck home in El Tigre.

"Your time is running sort of short, kid," said El Tigre. "Better run along while you got a chance."

"I've asked you a question."

"If you stay a while longer, you'll be eating lead by the way of answers."

"I'll take the chance with the lead then."

"You fool!" But El Tigre, having raised himself upon one elbow, sank back again with a gasp. "They'll kill you, Peter!" he breathed. "Don't you understand?"

"You old hound," said Peter Quince through his teeth. "What's the trick, you murdering, sneaking, crooked cut-throat, what's the trick behind it all?"

The wounded man groaned, but rather with despair and sorrow than anger at these insults.

"If you wish to get away with a free skin—go quickly, Peter!"

"I'll stay here."

"Peter!"

"You talk," sneered Peter, "as if you had a right to command me!"

"I have," said the outlaw. "I have a right, though I may have throwed it away. But, if there's no other way to move you, I'll tell you the truth: it's your father that's telling you to go, Peter."

It crumpled Peter Quince against the tall rocks behind him.

"Your father, Peter," went on the other slowly, reading answers in the horrified face of the youngster. "Your murdering, throat-cutting father! Will you go when he tells you to?"

But Peter slumped to his knees beside the giant and rested his hands upon the shoulders of El Tigre, so that he could peer the more closely. It was too terrible and strange not to be true. Had there been a physical resemblance between the two of them, it would have been easy to disbelieve, but they were so unlike that he knew El Tigre could not be lying to achieve an effect. Yet his reason still fought against the admission; for his head was spinning with wild thoughts.

"My father died eighteen years ago!" cried Peter.

The other shook his head.

"They gave me this," he said, and pointed to a great white blotch of a scar against his throat. "But I crawled away and managed to live through it. And finally I came out safe and sound. I headed for Mexico, and I've stayed here ever since!"

"You left me to manage as best I could?" asked Peter bitterly.

"No, no! From up the hillside I saw where they'd set fire to the house. And I took it for granted that they had burned you with the rest of the house. I thought that was the end of my old life—and that was why I went to a new country."

It was impossible to doubt.

"Suppose I had shot an inch lower!" breathed Peter. "Thank Heaven that kept me from that!"

"If you'd shot an inch lower," said John Quincy, "you'd have never carried the same load of your father's past on your shoulders."

"Don't say it!" groaned Peter. "Whatever you've done,

I've seen you take your chance with death rather than fight back against your son."

"You're not ashamed of me, Peter?"

"If I had my pick among all the fathers in the world, I'd choose you against them all!"

"They've put a price on my head, Peter."

"There's a price on mine. We'll live together and work together!"

"You'd come with me, boy?"

"What could keep me away?"

And then Peter looked hastily away, for he saw tears rush into the eyes of El Tigre, and the sight weakened and saddened him.

"Go back at once. When I'm riding again I'll come for you, Peter. Go back and tell Monterey that you dropped me but that my men herded you away."

The face of Peter darkened.

"Will you talk to me about one thing, Father?"

"About anything in my life."

"Why have you been trying to take the girl away?"

"What story has Monterey told you about that?"

"A story which—which rang very true." He spoke hesitatingly, but evidently he wished to give his father every chance to tell only the truth.

"A story that Monterey told would be sure to ring pretty true," said his father thoughtfully. "Because—lift me up and fold my coat and put it under my shoulders."

He closed his eyes and controlled his expression while Peter Quince obeyed. He made of the coat a pad to raise the elder man's shoulders from the ground. Then John Quincy nodded.

"That's better."

"Dad," muttered Peter, "this is agony for you. Every breath you draw is agony!"

"Not a bit," answered the older man. "Not a bit. That slug out of your gun slid off my ribs like a drop of water off of greased paper. It knocked me out, and the bleeding has sort of made me weak. But I'm coming back fast. I'll be riding inside of ten days and—but let's get back to Monterey. Gimme a cigarette to start on."

With deft fingers Peter Quince rolled a smoke and placed it between the lips of his father. Then he lighted it and leaned over John Quincy, watching him smoke, with a peculiar and ineffable pleasure. He felt that every instant spent in the company of this man was making him infinitely richer. He had reclaimed something worth far more than gold. And he watched his father in a quiet content. There were tears close to his eyes. Sometimes his lips trembled, and he felt a great rising desire to pour out his strength and his life to serve this battered man.

"My guns!" said Peter suddenly. "I thought a while ago that I'd be the happiest man in the world if I could drive a bullet through you, and now I'm the happiest person in the world because here you are in peace—talking to me. Go on, Dad!"

The other laid a hand on his arm, pressed it and went on with his tale. And, as he talked, from time to time he had to make a pause and control a twinge of pain. But always he went on steadily in his deep, slow voice. But Peter Quince sat back against the rocks, watching the moving lips, perhaps rising to offer a drink of water or a taste of brandy from the flask, according as it seemed to him that his father might need it.

30.   JOHN QUINCY TALKS

"THE WRONG that Monterey done was a big wrong," said John Quincy, "because when a good man does a wrong thing it's always a big wrong. Understand?"

"Monterey is a good man then?" muttered Peter Quince.

"He's a good man," nodded the father.

"He seemed to me—"

"Well, what?"

"He seemed to me to be rather smooth, rather crooked."

"What's wrong with him? Is he close-fisted?"

"Oh, no."

"Is he cruel?"

"I suppose not."

"What is it?"

"Nothing I can put my finger on," admitted Peter Quince. "But I'm afraid of him."

"There you have it," answered his father. "When a good man goes wrong he changes clear down to the bottom, and he becomes a pile worse'n the worst of the bad ones. Monterey was the finest man that ever stepped. He done a wrong thing, and it poisoned him. But he kept the face of a man that's good. That's what makes him dangerous now. I'll tell you the story."

He paused with closed eyes to recall the details. Then he said:

"When I left the States I went straight south with anger burning in the insides of me. I was a sick man. I'd seen my wife die and I'd seen my little boy burned alive, as I thought."

He stared at Peter hungrily.

"You got her face, lad," he said softly. "Seeing you, I see the kid I lost, and I see my poor girl, too! But I'll keep away from that. I can't—I can't stand it! And right then I knew that I couldn't stand it. I knew that if I stayed around in the States after that thing had been done to my blood and kin, I'd be doing some killings. They'd charged plenty of murders up to me in the States before that time. But what they charged me with was all lies. All lies, son! When a man is outlawed—when a man is fool enough not to stand his trial and gets outlawed—then everything that happens within a hundred miles of him is charged up to him.

"If it's knowed that he rides a bay hoss, then every hold-up artist that rides a bay hoss is called by his name, and every murder that men riding bay hosses do is added to his account. It'd been that way with me. But there was nothing but lies added agin me. Oh, they'd have hung me for them. They still would hang me. There's a hundred thousand good men would rub their hands and go to bed happy if they heard that I was burned alive. But God knows the truth about me!"

The blood of Peter Quince turned cold as the big man looked up. Yet it was not hypocrisy, as he could see at a glance. An explanation followed in solemn tones.

"Living the way I've lived, between the devil and the blue sky, with these here mountains pressing the soul of a man up against the cold of the stars by night—why, a gent has sure got to begin thinking about the power that made him. And that's the way it's been with me. God ain't knowed me, but I've knowed Him. I've done mighty wild things. But there ain't been a time when I ain't tried to help the ones that was down and grind only them that was up. I've taken nothing from poor men. They've taken everything from me. I've made hundreds and thousands of dollars. Where's it gone? I staked five hundred men and women and babies when the town of San Triste burned, and they was turned out. That was one thing that I've done. There've been others. I've given it to my men. But take my wallet now, and you'll find it pretty near empty. As for the killings, I've never fought except where I was cornered, and I've never drawn first on another human being. I've done harm, but I dunno just how the books will be balanced when I come to my accounting."

Peter Quince nodded. He was drawing in great breaths, as though these words were purifying water that washed him clean of taint and restored to him a good name.

"When I left the States I rode south as fast as I could, afraid of myself, not them that was chasing me—afraid that I'd turn back on 'em and smash 'em to pulp and bones! I wanted to crush out lives like wine makers crush grapes.

"So I come to the Rio Grande and rode through, and on the other side I started over again. There wasn't more than one thing that I could do. That was to start the same game that I'd tried in the North. That's what some of the boys told me that I met here south of the border— men that I'd knowed in the old days on the range. They told me that I couldn't go straight, but I tried to fool them.

"I started in prospecting, hit it rich right off, cleaned up with a good sale, and found myself in Mexico City three months after I crossed the river. In the city I picked up with a young couple, a young miner and his wife. Their name was Sanborn. There was John Sanborn, the husband, and Kate Sanborn, the wife. Kate was going to have a baby.

"They'd come away in from the mines so that Kate could have the advantage of a good doctor and all that. And the first thing that they done was to get rid of all their money. So I floated them along through. I was flush, and the coin didn't mean nothing to me. In the meantime, I was taking a lot of interest in what was going on. You'd have thought that the world was going to make a new start on account of that baby that was coming. And when it arrived, it sure was an up-to-date, one-hundred-per-cent kid. It was a girl, and they named it Mary."

"What!" cried Peter.

"Don't get ahead of my story, son!"

"You don't mean to say—"

"Wait a minute, kid! Things went sure enough fine for ten days. Then Kate Sanborn got a back-set. In three hours she was dead with pneumonia. That was the first lightning stroke.

"But there was still a father left to take care of little Mary. More'n that—when her mother lay dying she'd told me that John was plumb helpless with a kid, and she asked me to promise that little Mary would be taken care of. And I swore to her that I'd see that she got what was right for her! I swore that, and a promise means a considerable lot to me. Today I turned loose a man that was sticking to a promise he'd made, even though the promise was a bad one!

"But one day, when I come home with an armful of toys for the kid, I come in to find John Sanborn raving and raging through the place. He tackled me and tried to shoot me up—swore that I'd done the job. I asked him what, and he said that little Mary had been stolen.

"It knocked me all of a heap. She sure was a fine enough kid for anybody to have wanted to steal, but it never occurred to me that there was anybody in the world low enough to—but let that go with the rest. I sure didn't know much those days!

"John Sanborn went pretty near crazy. I offered a thousand dollars' reward. The police done what they could by way of a search, but there wasn't no trace of Mary brought to light. She'd been left lying in her crib, with the nurse sitting and sewing in the next room, with an open door in between. In ten minutes Mary was stole. We found the tracks that showed how the thief had come in through the window and took the kid away.

"Sanborn started drinking, got into a drunken knife fight, and had his heart split in two. That was the end of

Mary's father and mother. Then I hit out after the skunks that had murdered John, and I got into a pack of trouble myself, that wound up with me kiting off through the mountains, emptying a rifle at the posse that was a-following me. However, I was used to that way of living.

"What I done in the next five years don't amount to much, leastwise for this here story. But when I got through with my work I was pretty well knowed through the length and breadth of Mexico, and the rurales had near busted their hearts twenty times trying to get me. But at the fag end of the five years, as I was jogging along up Monterey Valley one day, I come through the woods and into a clearing, and there I seen little Mary a-playing!" He paused and drew a great breath. Peter was frozen with attention.

"There wasn't no doubt about it," went on the outlaw. "She had all of her father in her face and something more. It was so plumb clear that all I needed was to find a photograph of him to use as evidence in a court of law. It would have convicted Monterey sure enough.

"Not down here in Mexico, though. The Montereys are plumb worshipped all through these parts, and they got a right to be. They've been Providence and then some to the poor and sick for a hundred miles any direction you ride from Casa Monterey. Well, son, I thought of all of them things while I was a-sitting in the saddle and looking down in the face of the kid.

"Then she sees me and gives a yell, and I rode off into the shadow of the trees. And the nurse seen me and gives a yell, too. But I wasn't ready to act. I wanted to get a lot of information before I done anything.

"That night I got back to my gang, and I picked out the best man I had, an old fellow that couldn't handle a gun or a knife because he'd got the palsy. But he was worth millions of dollars to go in ahead of a job and get the information and lay the plant for the rest of us. I sent him into the Monterey valley to find out what he could about that little girl.

"He comes back inside of twenty-four hours with everything that I wanted to know. Took him a whole hour to tell the story that he'd heard right from the lips of the baby's own nurse.

"I'll give you the short of it: Monterey's widowed sister comes down from the States and he takes her to Mexico City, where her baby's born. She's mighty sick—so sick that the baby can't be showed to her for a whole two weeks. Mark you that, son! Not for a whole two weeks! And then up comes a day when the doctor says that the little baby has to be brought in, because the mother is grieving about missing the kid's face. And in comes a fine little baby girl, healthy as can be—which was mighty strange, says nurse, seeing that the mother was so sick when the kid was born!"

"Very strange!" nodded Peter Quince, remembering the tale which had been told him before about the birth of Mary.

"Too strange to be true," said John Quincy, "and it was all that I needed to make me know that the Mary I'd seen in the forest was the Mary that was the daughter of Kate Sanborn—the Mary that I'd sworn to take care of!

"And there she was being raised up in a family that didn't have no right to her and never taught her a word about her true mother and father. You understand? I lay awake groaning and worrying about it. Then I seen that I'd be haunted by poor Kate Sanborn's face the whole rest of my life unless I found out some sort of a way to take that little girl away from them and raise her up to look back to her rightful father and mother instead of Monterey's sister. You see?

"But how was I to raise that kid among the mountains? I'll tell you what I done. I made the biggest raid that I ever worked. I buried the coin I took and waited for a chance. Then I bought a boat—or had one bought for me—and had that boat laid in at a cove on the coast ready to sail out to sea—a little sloop, mind you! When I had that fixed I go right back to Monterey Valley and wait for my chance to get the girl. My plan was to take her away through the mountains, slide down to the cove, where I had the boat all ready and waiting, and then to go down the coast until I got to a South American port. There I'd get a steamer for Europe. In Europe, I'd settle down and raise Mary by the right name of Mary Sanborn and make her a lady as proud and as fine as ever stepped." His enthusiasm shone in his eyes and rang in his voice. "Because she was a little lady even at five. She kept her head as high and her voice as low as any princess, son!"

"I'll wager she did!" murmured Peter Quince, looking far off and seeing the picture as clearly as if he himself had painted it.

"So I come down out of the mountains, and on the lucky day I got hold of Mary and scooted up the valley and into the mountains, holding her in my arms. But there wasn't no good fortune waiting for me that day. There wasn't no good fortune at all!" He hesitated and then closed his eyes with a groan. "A sharp wind come and spread the clouds between me and the sun. And then, all in a minute, you might say, there was a storm cutting at my face. I looked down to Mary.

" 'Are you scared?' says I to her.

"But she looks back up to me like an owl, quiet and not saying a word. I ride on for a while longer.

" 'Are you near frozen, honey?' says I to her.

"But she just turns up her eyes to me as calm as could be, and by the Lord, Peter, she smiled! Her face was all pinched and blue, but she managed to smile. I suppose that she thought it was all a game, and that I was a sort of a man-sized playmate for her!

"Well, son, it near broke my heart when I seen that smile. I seen that I couldn't win that day. The storm was bad on me. It would be death on her. So I laid her aside, safe and sound, and rode on, and I felt that I'd left something behind me that was like a piece out of my soul. For all the time I was a-holding her, it was like I was holding my own boy, Peter, that was about her age when I seen him last."

His voice died away. He added later: "That's the whole story. I've kept trying to get at her, and I've always failed!

"That's why I followed poor Martin Avery. A spy of mine had seen him get into a secret passage at Casa Monterey. The next day Avery fled—rather, he fled at night. And Monterey had him followed. I knowed that Avery had seen more than he was supposed to have any sort of right to see, and so I come down and followed him to the tavern and grabbed him. I took him away to make more talk.

"But the boy had honor, and I couldn't torture him. I hadn't the heart for that. Just the same, I know that he could give proof that even one of the courts down in this part of the country would have to take to show that Mary should be called Sanborn!"

So the story came to an end, and Peter sat for a long moment in thought.

"Father," he said at last, "have you any belief in fate?"

"I dunno," said John Quincy.

"Well," said Peter, "there's fate in this one thing. You've worked all these years to help Mary, thinking that I was dead. And I've been tangled up, one after the other, with six girls, all named Mary—and the seventh one is this one. And the seventh one, Father, is the girl I'm to marry, or else die in the trying!"

31. THE REBUFF

THEY DID not rush Peter Quince when his ten minutes were ended. Instead, the voice of the leader called them in, and they were presented, one after another, to his son. Peter Quince strove to explain how only the clemency of his father had permitted him to send a bullet into the body of the older man, but El Tigre frowned him down, and the banditti stared at the two with dumb wonder. They had looked upon El Tigre as a man more terrible than his namesake. That he would have a son even more formidable finished off the picture of his own qualities. They knew that Ranjel Verial had gone down before the gun of this slender and handsome youth. Now their great leader was fallen. It was not the condemnation of El Tigre—it was simply the glorification of Don Peter.

"Señor," said Guillermo, "I have a little token to give you when we part. It is a small thing, but one which I wish you may keep to remember me by and always to know that I am at your service!"

So saying, he pulled a broad Mexican peso out of his pocket, tossed it ten yards away in the air, and knocked it into a glimmering streak with a revolver bullet. He picked it up and brought it back to Peter. A large hole was bitten cleanly out of one side, and the newly exposed metal glistened.

"It is for you," said Guillermo.

"You are a thousand times kind," said Peter.

But Guillermo had simply set an example, not accomplished something unique. Another clipped with a slug of lead a twig off a branch and gave Peter the bit of wood. Another shot a knife into a slender sapling, wrenched it out, and gave Peter the knife itself. In fifty seconds there was not a man in the lot who had not made Peter a present of some sort, and every present was a token of prowess. There was something as childlike as impressive about this performance, but Peter accepted everything with a solemn face of gratitude. As a matter of fact, he saw that it was giving him the allegiance of a band of men as formidable, perhaps, as any in the universe.

He said good-bye to his father and swung into the saddle on Bad Luck. He headed away toward Monterey Valley once more, with the whole story which he was to tell the great señor planned. He rehearsed that tale on the way, and as he rode his confidence grew. He was as certain that he was to win the seventh Mary as he was that he breathed and lived at that moment. He was as certain that Mary could not stand up against his brains and the power of his father's band as he was that a child cannot stand before a man.

But when he found himself in Monterey Valley again, his heart changed. He was in the center of a kingdom, and his hand was against the king. It was not a question of tens and twenties that would be opposed to him. It was a matter of thousands of fighters who would struggle at the bidding of Monterey. And he remembered, too, that as capable a man as his father had been attempting for nearly fifteen years to do what he hoped to accomplish in an instant.

It was a bit preposterous.

Therefore, it was a sober youth who rode into the valley of Monterey and wandered up toward the big house on the cliff. But he did not need to go all the way. He met the señor and Mary swinging down the road at a long gallop. They drew up at the sight of him, and Peter watched the señor grow pale with excitement as he came closer.

"The news!" cried Monterey.

Peter raised his hat to the girl.

"No luck!" said Peter.

"Thank heaven!" breathed Mary.

"What did you say?" asked Monterey sharply.

"I can't help it," she answered. "I can't help remembering that day when he caught me up and rode me into the storm. I felt that time that he would have died to make me happy. And, in spite of everything, there's a warm spot in my heart for him."

"Because he didn't take you and let you freeze?" exclaimed Monterey.

"I suppose it boils down to that," she said, a little thoughtfully.

"And you?" asked the señor very shortly, turning upon Peter.

"I met El Tigre."

"Oh!"

This was from Mary.

"I met him and had the good luck—"

"You killed the hound, Quince!"

"Only wounded him!"

"By heavens," murmured Monterey, "then I was right after all. When I first heard of you something spoke up inside of me—something told me that here was another man of the same breed—"

This was so close to dangerous ground that Peter stared at him. Of course, it had been an unconscious hit.

"Tell me every word of it!" panted the señor.

"But he—he's still alive?" urged Mary.

"Still living." And Peter thanked her for that kindness with a smile. "I had that luck in the draw. El Tigre went down, but he was only wounded. It left me in a predicament."

"But why? But why? There was the man in your hands —in your hands and helpless!" cried the señor, striking his palms together in an ecstasy of impatience.

"I'll tell you. He was too badly wounded to take him away on a horse—in fact, his own horse had run away. My hands were tied in that respect."

"But where was the trouble in the whole affair? I don't see it," said the señor.

"But, you understand, my shot had gone angling through his body—"

"Horrible!" breathed Mary.

The lips of Monterey merely twitched, and he kept his fascinated glance fixed upon the narrator.

"He was in such a shape that he had to be taken care of or he might have bled to death. So I had to make camp and take care of him as well as I could."

Monterey threw his arms wildly above his head.

"Madness! Madness!" he cried.

And, at this token of his rage, half a dozen riders, mounted upon fine horses, who had been following them down road as a sort of rear guard to the master and the mistress, drew closer, putting their hands to their weapons and eyeing Peter.

Monterey's voice rang out.

"Why not let him bleed to death? Why not shorten the process by driving your knife through his murderous throat?"

And Peter Quince, watching the convulsed face of his companion, remembered what his father had said—that when a good man turns bad he becomes worse than the worst. There was no doubt that Monterey meant all that he said and more. His whole body was trembling with his passion.

"I couldn't do that," said Peter slowly.

"You mean to say you had him in your power—and then you let him escape from your idiot hands? Take him —in the name of reason take this fool from me."

He stifled with his fury and made a gesture to the guard to obey him. There was no question of resistance. Before Peter could have drawn a gun the ready weapons of the men covered him. He would have been blown out of the saddle by a torrent of lead had he so much as lifted a hand. Therefore, very wisely, he sat still and smiled at the infuriated Monterey.

Then he looked at the girl. It was vastly important to

see how she took this proceeding, and it was plain to discover that she was taking it very, very ill. She had lost color, save for one bright spot which was burning in either cheek, and she was biting her lip to keep from speaking what must have been in her mind. She only said: "Uncle Felipe, would you really have had him kill a wounded man who was helpless?"

"Who calls El Tigre a man?" thundered Monterey. "I am only angry because this fool had a snake's head under his heel and then refused to crush it! Take him back to the house. Keep him there carefully. I have yet to make up my mind about him!"

"Uncle Felipe!"

"What is it?"

"But I know that this is all a jest! You don't mean that you'll mistreat him for no fault?"

"Stupidity is the worst crime in the world!"

"I know that you'll not harm him or detain him for an instant," said Mary. And under her eye Monterey changed color a little, as though he realized that he had gone too far and exposed his mind too much to the girl.

"You are free to go," he said stiffly to Peter Quince. "But never come back. Somewhere under this affair there is treason. I say that I smell the treason in it!"

"Give me five minutes to explain!" pleaded Peter.

"Not five seconds."

"How can you be so unreasonable, Uncle Felipe?"

"Unreasonable? You don't know this fellow, Mary. He may not have beaten El Tigre, as he claims, but he is almost formidable enough to have done so. And his whole past is a long record of crimes. Murdering men and philandering with women have been his two chief pursuits!"

He had struck at the very weakest point in Peter's armor. He felt the shaft enter, and he looked quickly at the girl to see how desperately he had been wounded in her estimation. Her head had gone higher indeed. Her smile had frozen in place. He found himself snatched a thousand leagues from his goal.

"But if you come again," Monterey was saying, "you may expect to find my valley and my house dangerous. I suspect you, señor. And I shall act upon suspicion if you come into my hands again."

So Peter turned his horse and rode slowly down the valley up which he had come so gaily and with desperately high hopes. He let Bad Luck jog away as slowly as he pleased, and behind him he heard the voice of Monterey saying: "I have made myself a great deal of trouble for the future. I prophesy it now. I have not seen the last of that young man!"

And Mary answered: "I earnestly hope that we have!"

32.   AN AFTER-DINNER CALL

A SWIFT month passed over Monterey Valley. It was a quick month because the air was filled with happy content, and happy days are the ones which leave no mark behind them. El Tigre was gone. He had neither been seen nor heard of for weeks. Twice, to be sure, a band which seemed much like the force of the famous desperado had made pillaging expeditions, but in both cases they had struck on the farther side of the mountains. Monterey Valley seemed to be given up by the freebooter.

But if time passed easily and pleasantly for the tenants of Monterey, for the señor himself the time was slow and painful. Now he found himself surrounded by an air of gloom in Mary. It grew in her day by day. To be sure, she was as amiable as ever; she was as willing to ride or hunt with him; she would walk through the mountains with him as ever. And yet the señor detected a great difference. Half of her heart was turned away to other things, and he finally put his trouble into words.

They were finishing their dinner, sitting quietly opposite one another in the great old hall, Monterey drinking coffee and smoking cigarettes, and Mary watching him with her hands folded in her lap. Once these had been the best moments of the day to Monterey, when he sat with the girl at the end of its activities and talked over with her what had been done, what luck they had had in their hunting, what they had seen in their rides, or the breaking of a new horse, or a plan for a garden of new flowers, or a thousand other things, for he had made her a partner in all the happiness of his life. But tonight he said: "Why are you so unhappy, Mary?"

She started, and glanced at him with what she intended should be surprise only, but she could not keep the guilt from creeping in.

"You see," he explained, to keep her from the embarrassment of a protest which must be overridden. "I have been watching you for all these days. It seems an eternity of time to me since I have seen you happy. And tonight I can stand no more of it without trying to get at the reason. What is the reason, Mary? Why do you listen to me with your ears only and keep your eyes and your mind fixed on something a thousand miles behind me?"

She was dressed in some white stuff whose name Monterey did not know, but it had the sheen of satin together with the translucent softness of a thin silk; and over her shoulders there was a wrap which was a flush of color rather than a protection against weather, so fine was that veil woven. She dropped her face upon one thin hand to consider what he had said, and the hand caught up a hundred filmy wrinkles of the veils, and the rosy color deepened to a blush along her cheek and her throat.

"I suppose I'm a little tired," she said. "Sometimes that makes one seem thoughtful."

"You're not tired," said Monterey.

"Oh, but how can you be so sure of that?"

"Because you are as strong as a whiplash. You see that I know you, Mary, better than I know myself. Come, come, I've walked too many mountain trails with you not to know that such things as you've done today are not even exercise for you."

She was taken off her guard in the effort to find another angle to the question.

"All weariness is not of the muscles," she said. And then she bit her lip and stared at him, but she saw him whiten and grow old of face.

"I didn't mean that, of course!" she whispered. "I was merely hunting for another side to the argument."

Instead of answering at once he made it a thousand times harder for her by pausing to sip his coffee again, and in a mental agony she watched him raise the delicate little cup, as transparent as an eggshell, and she watched the coffee tilt across the border of gold which inlaid its lip. Finally he said:

"What has happened, Mary?"

"Nothing," she said miserably.

"Please!" he urged her.

"It is really nothing. I'm happy, Uncle Felipe. I'm very happy. Why shouldn't I be?"

"I've asked myself that a thousand times during the past week. Heaven knows if there is anything I can give you! You have only to ask me, my dear."

"Uncle Felipe!" she cried. "You break my heart when you talk of giving me more. More? Oh, no! What could I have? I have twenty horses to ride, I have two maids, I have more rooms than I know what to do with—and furnished with all that a heart could desire. I have silks and laces and jewels; I have paintings and books. What more could any girl in the world want?"

"You say that, Mary, feeling in your heart of hearts that I should understand at once that all of these things are nothing compared with something else of which I have robbed you. But I am dull tonight. I have no imagination. Tell me what that other thing may be."

His tone was pleading.

"I don't understand," said Mary.

"I see that we are drifting apart," sighed Monterey. "And do you know that sometimes I trace the change in you back to the day which young Peter Quince spent with us?"

"Bah!" cried Mary. "Just his name is all I need to make me very angry! Peter Quince?"

"You were fond of him while he was here."

"He was so handsome," she admitted carelessly. "But when I found out what he was—a murderer and a philanderer—I only wondered that you ever allowed him to come into the house."

"Because I was striving to get rid of our mutual plague and enemy, El Tigre. As for Peter Quince—"

"Yes, what became of him?"

"Are you eager to know?"

"I hope that justice overtook him at the last."

"He has joined El Tigre."

"After trying to kill him!"

"I suppose that would not be so hard. As a matter of fact, he probably got El Tigre at a disadvantage, and then the wily old scoundrel bought off Peter with fair promises. Isn't that probable?"

"He was only a boy. Could he possibly have beaten a terrible destroyer such as El Tigre?"

"He was like a great cat—that Peter Quince.

"Ah, yes," said Mary, in such a voice that her uncle glanced critically at her, but he found her looking vaguely into space.

"But to think that he would actually have joined the outlaw he went out to fight!" she said at last.

"Of course, Quince was only a rascal."

"Of course," she murmured. "And yet—"

"Well?"

"He is so young a man. It seems strange, don't you think, that such a young man should be such a bad one?"

"Strange, but very true. When he was—"

"Let's talk of something else," she broke in eagerly. "When I think that that terrible man was actually in this house—and that he sat at this very table—and that we have talked and smiled at him—why, I'm ashamed of you, Uncle Felipe!"

He shrugged his shoulders.

"Such a rascal shall never get in again, you may be sure of that!"

"What is that noise?" asked Mary suddenly. "Is Pedro coming back?"

"Nothing could bring him back," said the master, shaking his head. "All the servants know that after the dinner is ended they must leave the dining room in absolute quiet. I have seen too many of the most fascinating after-dinner conversations ruined by the promiscuous entrance of servants."

"And yet I heard something at the lock," said Mary. "At least I thought that I did!"

"There could not have been a hand on the lock."

"Ah!" breathed the girl.

He saw the terror in her eyes and, turning from his chair, found himself facing one of the doors which had opened and revealed the dapper form of Peter Quince standing in the aperture. Peter stepped in, with a taller man behind him, who closed the door, turned the latch and, facing them, revealed the formidable countenance of El Tigre himself!

33.   "STRAIGHT AS A SWORD"

"THE BELL—the bell!" gasped Mary.

The fumbling foot of Monterey found the button beneath the table and ground down upon it until the knob crushed his foot through the thin sole of the shoe. But there was not the familiar answering murmur in the distance.

"The bell cord is cut," said Peter Quince. "We looked to that, as a matter of course, before we came in. And now it remains for us to lock all the doors."

He suited action to the word, passing rapidly from door to door and making them fast from the inside, while he removed the keys and dropped them into his pocket. In the meantime, El Tigre did not move from the first position which he had assumed near the door. His right hand hung at his hip, resting there easily above the butt of his six-shooter, and, although the fingers did not stir toward the butt of the weapon, there needed no telling that he was ready to draw and fire at the first opening. At any distance in that room his revolver play would be as sure as death, and Señor Monterey admitted defeat.

"What is it?" he asked, with only a little huskiness to tell that he was moved. "What insanity can have made you dare to come here, El Tigre?"

El Tigre raised his hand. It imposed silence at once.

"He planned things out," he said, indicating Peter. "And he'll do the talking about it."

In the meantime, Peter had drawn the curtains in the room. Then he approached the table.

"We've thought matters over from every angle," he said. "We hoped for a while to take the house with a rush. But, when you doubled the number of the armed men around the house, we knew that the job would be too much for us."

"I ask only one thing," pleaded the señor. "Tell me what traitor you bought up? Who was the hound who let you in?"

"You will know in a few minutes at the most—or else you will not be in a position to know anything. The man is Juan Garien. He is no longer a member of your household, but of the household of El Tigre."

"Has El Tigre a household?"

"After the government has pardoned him in full, he will set one up."

"A pardon for El Tigre? I cannot help a smile, señor"

"Smile as you please. Can you imagine no one with influence enough to secure his pardon from the government?"

"No one!"

"Not even Felipe Monterey?"

"That is possible, I suppose, if Felipe Monterey chose to intercede for him."

"The señor will choose to do that," said the young man calmly. "He will do his best to win a pardon for El Tigre!"

Monterey leaned back in his chair, smiling.

"You have come here hoping to do something with great talk. But in that you are a thousand times wrong. I cannot be budged. And as for you, you will be filled with lead before you leave the house."

"Wrong again. We can leave as we entered."

"Listen!" said Monterey.

They stood stiffly silent, and then they heard it, that soft and penetrating noise which passes through thick walls—the whisper of shuffling feet over stone flagging. Scores of feet were scurrying into the hall.

El Tigre, with an exclamation which was like a snarl, cried: "I told you, Peter! We've put our heads in the lion's mouth!"

"The lion has no teeth," answered Peter calmly. "We are here with him. Our revolvers are the keys with which we must unlock the doors of our danger here. The señor dies if the least finger is raised against us!"

The last words were a ringing shout to warn those who

were scurrying in the hall outside, and there was a groan for answer.

"What can you wish?" asked Monterey, frowning, as the other side of the picture was brought to his attention.

"For fifteen years," said Peter, "El Tigre has been trying to reach Mary."

"Well?"

"To tell her the truth about her parentage!"

There was a sharp exclamation from Monterey. He fell back into the chair from which he had started up, his face bloodless.

"What fiend came out of hell to tell you of that thing?" he groaned to Peter Quince.

But now Mary was on her knees beside Monterey, catching at his hands.

"What does it mean?" moaned the girl. "That your sister was not my— Does it mean that?"

"I am choking," gasped Monterey. "No, no, my dear. It doesn't mean that! It only means that—they they are lying! They will try to prove that my sister's child died at birth, and that you were stolen."

"We have claimed nothing," said Peter. "You have damned yourself with your own words, Monterey!"

Monterey groaned as he realized that emotion had betrayed him. Then he turned hastily to Mary, but she was rising to her feet, and she pushed herself away from him.

"Uncle Felipe!" she said. "Oh, I have dreamed it, and the dream was true all the time!"

"Be silent, Mary. I admit nothing. They have come here only with lies."

But, to his utter amazement, she whirled suddenly from him and ran across the room to Peter Quince.

"Peter, Peter!" she cried. "Tell me all the truth quickly!"

"I shall! Will you trust what I tell you?"

"If you look me straight in the eye—straight as a sword, Peter, I'd trust you as you talk! Who were my true father and mother?"

"Kate and John Sanborn."

There was an involuntary groan from Monterey which confirmed everything. "They are both dead, Mary," he added softly.

"Oh, Peter," she whispered, "my head is spinning. What shall I do?"

"Dear—only hold fast to me and listen!"

And, as she clung to him, weeping softly, she heard the drawling voice of El Tigre—how unchanged since the day he had carried her away in the storm—saying:

"And Peter has figured it out that there ain't anything to hate you for, Monterey. I'd like to carve your heart out, but he says that you ain't to blame. You started doing it for your sister's sake. And you can square up with me by getting my pardon from the government—you understand, señor?"

There was no answer from Monterey. He lay face downward on the table, his hands clutching at the cloth.

Peter's lips brushed Mary's hair.